Best Friend or Worst Enemy?

"You want to rub it in Ellen Ming's face that her father is under suspicion," Brittany told Kim.

"Aren't you being a little hypocritical, Brittany?" Kim responded. "You're putting the whole story in the *Record.*"

"I don't know if the story is going in the *Record* or not," Brittany snapped.

"You're just upset because your darling Chip Worthington hasn't called you," Kim said spitefully. "I saw the way you threw yourself at him at the dance. It's a good thing you don't have much of a gag reflex. He's awfully hard to swallow, isn't he?"

Samantha pressed her fingers against her temples. "Will you two stop it, please? I'm getting a headache. All you do these days is argue."

"All right," Brittany muttered.

What did it matter? Soon Chip would be hers. So what if Brittany wasn't sure if she liked him or not? Kim couldn't stand him, and that would drive her absolutely nuts!

Books in the River Heights ™ Series

#1 Love Times Three
#2 Guilty Secrets
#3 Going Too Far
#4 Stolen Kisses
#5 Between the Lines
#6 Lessons in Love
#7 Cheating Hearts
#8 The Trouble with Love
#9 Lies and Whispers

Available from ARCHWAY Paperbacks

LIES AND WHISPERS

CAROLYN KEENE

AN ARCHWAY PAPERBACK
Published by POCKET BOOKS
New York London Toronto Sydney Tokyo Singapore

This book is a work of fiction. Names, characters, places and incidents are either the product of the author's imagination or are used fictitiously. Any resemblance to actual events or locales or persons, living or dead, is entirely coincidental.

AN ARCHWAY PAPERBACK *Original*

An Archway Paperback published by
POCKET BOOKS, a division of Simon & Schuster
1230 Avenue of the Americas, New York, NY 10020

Produced by Mega-Books of New York, Inc.

ISBN: 0-671-73113-0

First Archway Paperback printing January 1991

10 9 8 7 6 5 4 3 2 1

Cover art by Carla Sormanti

Printed in the U.S.A.

IL 6+

LIES AND WHISPERS

1

"Hurry, Ben!" Lacey Dupree urged. "Can't you go any faster?"

"I'm doing the speed limit, Lacey," Ben Newhouse responded, frowning. His foot remained steady on the gas pedal as he drove through the dark, snowy streets of River Heights.

Lacey impatiently brushed back her halo of long red-gold hair and trained her eyes on the road ahead. Just one more block and they'd be at the hospital. One more block and she could see Rick Stratton, her boyfriend. Ben had rushed up to her at the Winter Carnival Ball to tell her that Rick had finally regained consciousness after a rock-climbing accident.

Ben made a left turn into the hospital

parking lot. There was a space right near the entrance, and he headed into it. Lacey opened her door as the car coasted to a stop.

"Whoa, Lacey!" Ben hit the brakes. He shifted into park and turned to her. "I know you're anxious, but take it easy, okay?"

"I'm sorry, Ben," Lacey said as she opened the door wider. "I just can't wait. I have to see Rick!" Her light blue eyes pleaded with him.

"All right," Ben said reluctantly. "Run on ahead. I'll catch up."

"Thanks, Ben," Lacey said gratefully. She slid out of the car and headed for the entrance.

"I'll wait down here for you," Ben said.

Lacey lifted her hand to acknowledge Ben's comment as she raced through the electric doors. She stopped at the front desk to ask for permission to see Rick after visiting hours. The doctor had left word for her to be admitted. Then she ran across the lobby and skidded to a stop in front of the bank of elevators.

Jabbing the up button impatiently, Lacey stopped to take a deep breath. Now that she was actually there, she started to worry again. What would Rick say when he saw her? He might hate her and blame her. If they hadn't had that terrible argument, he wouldn't have fallen during his rock-climbing expedition. He wouldn't have been lying unconscious in the hospital for more than two weeks!

The elevator doors slid open, and Lacey jumped on. She tapped her foot the whole time the elevator rose. As soon as the doors opened, she stepped out.

The corridor was deserted, and she heard her heels click hollowly as she made her way to Rick's room. She thought of how she'd come there, day after day, her heart breaking at the sight of Rick lying unconscious. The pain of it had been hard to bear. But how would it compare to the pain of Rick rejecting her now?

Rick's door was open. Lacey peeked in. Rick was talking to his mother in a low voice that sounded weak. His father and brother, Tom, sat on the far side of the bed. Rick was pale, and there were dark circles under his eyes. His muscular body seemed thin now. Even though he looked ill, Lacey thought, he'd never looked so good to her.

He glanced up just then. "Lacey," he said.

"Hello, Rick." Lacey couldn't seem to move from the doorway. Did he want her to go to him? Her eyes filled with tears. She didn't know what to do!

Suddenly Rick grinned. It was like a shadow of his old grin, but she saw the same flash of humor in his hazel eyes. "I'd get up, Lacey, but I don't think it would be too smart. I just might fall at your feet. Of course, that would be kind of romantic, but—"

"Oh, Rick." Laughing, Lacey ran across the room. Her eyes blurred with tears as she bent over to kiss him. For a moment she remembered how cold and still his lips had been when he was unconscious. She hid a small shiver as she straightened up again. "I'm so glad you're back," she whispered.

"Don't cry," he said. "This is a happy occasion."

"A very happy occasion," Mrs. Stratton said. She put her hand on Lacey's shoulder. Lacey turned and saw that she was crying, too. The two of them had spent so many hours together at Rick's bedside. Mr. Stratton and Tom smiled at her from the other side of Rick's hospital bed.

"I feel so badly that I wasn't here," Lacey said to Mrs. Stratton. "I had to be at the dance. I can't believe Rick woke up tonight, of all nights!"

"Did I interrupt your dancing?" Rick asked, his eyes twinkling.

"I didn't dance a step!" Lacey said,

shocked. Then she realized that Rick was teasing her. "I spilled punch all over everyone instead," she admitted.

"Is that what they're wearing to the Winter Carnival Ball these days?" Rick asked, indicating her plain black skirt and white blouse. "I thought it was a little more formal."

Lacey grinned. She couldn't bear to wear a formal dress or fix her hair for the ball, and she'd barely noticed what clothes she'd taken out of her closet. "I couldn't stand it without you," she said softly. She took his hand and squeezed it.

"Everything is going to be all right, Lacey," Rick said. His steady gaze held no anger, no secrets. He didn't blame her; she could tell that now. They would talk later, when they were alone, but right now the look on his face was enough.

Lacey gave her first real smile in weeks. "Everything's going to be just fabulous," she said.

Ellen Ming waited with Karen Jacobs outside River Heights High for her father. He had said he'd pick her up after the dance, and she had never known him to be late. It was after eleven now, and they were the last two waiting for a ride.

Karen leaned against the railing, staring

out at the parking lot and playing with a strand of her light brown hair. She'd been afraid earlier that Ben Newhouse, her boyfriend, had run off with Emily Van Patten, a beautiful model who was his ex-girlfriend. She'd been relieved when a friend told her that Ben had to drive Lacey Dupree to the hospital. But Karen still felt shaky. She'd confided in Ellen that she was convinced the gorgeous blond model was her rival. Now, instead of going to the Loft for pizza with Ben, Karen was stuck waiting for Mr. Ming with Ellen.

"Did you hear about Brittany and Tim?" Ellen asked her. She wanted to divert Karen's thoughts from Ben, and she thought some dirt about Karen's rival on the school paper might do the trick. Brittany Tate was gorgeous, smart, and devious. She'd played many an underhanded trick on Karen.

"No," Karen said listlessly.

"Nobody knows what happened, but Tim Cooper would hardly look at her all night. And after she'd finally gotten him to go out with her! Everyone's wondering if they had a fight," Ellen said.

She waited for Karen to speculate on what could have occurred. But Karen only shrugged. "I guess," she said. "We'll probably never know."

Ellen went back to silently looking for her father's car. Nothing she said seemed to help Karen's mood. Ellen had to admit she had a hard time sympathizing completely. Earlier that year, she'd had a big crush on Kevin Hoffman, the vice-president of the student council. For those few weeks she could plunge from the heights of excitement to the depths of despair in a matter of hours, depending on whether Kevin looked at her or gave her a grin across the room during a meeting. It had been a crazy time. She'd thought she'd been really depressed and upset some days, but now Ellen knew what *real* trouble was.

She pulled her ski cap down low over her thick black bangs and sighed. Things couldn't be worse around the Ming household. Her father and mother were barely speaking—they walked around the house like zombies. Ellen and her sister, Suzanne, were beginning to fear the worst. They were afraid that any day now their parents would sit them down and announce they were getting a divorce.

Ellen almost wished that it would happen soon. The suspense was killing her. The night before, she'd come home late and found her father sitting in the living room all alone in the dark. He'd been smoking a cigarette, and he'd quit ten years ago! Ellen had suddenly become frightened by this change in her father. She'd run upstairs and burst into tears in her room.

The Mings' car swung into the school parking lot and pulled up beside a shoveled-out spot on the sidewalk.

"He's here," Ellen said, relief flooding her voice. Finally she ran down the steps toward the car with Karen.

"Hi, Dad," she said as she slid into the front seat.

"Hi, Mr. Ming," Karen greeted him from the back seat.

"Hello, girls. Sorry I'm late. How was the dance?"

"Okay," Ellen said. Karen didn't answer. "The gym looked fabulous, but all the snowflakes started to fall off the walls by the end of the night. Sasha Lopez was running around with glue all over her fingers."

"That's nice," Mr. Ming said. He frowned at the traffic light ahead of him.

Ellen bit her lip. Her father was never like this. He always listened to her. In fact, he loved to hear her gossip after a dance. He wasn't like other fathers. He would volunteer to chauffeur Ellen and Suzanne so that he could keep track of their busy lives, and he was always ready to talk to them about school, about *anything*. Now he wasn't even listening to her!

Ellen made a resolution. She would ask her father that very night what was wrong. She'd *make* him tell her.

But after they dropped Karen off, Ellen couldn't seem to get the question out. Her father seemed so far away. He pulled into the driveway and turned off the ignition. For a minute he just sat there.

Ellen opened her door, then stuck her head back in. "Dad? Are you coming?"

Mr. Ming nodded. "Right."

They walked toward the front door together. Finally, as Mr. Ming turned the knob, Ellen got up the courage to speak.

"Dad? Could we talk a minute?"

He sighed. "Could it wait until tomorrow, sweetie? Your mom and I are scheduled for a discussion ourselves."

"Sure," Ellen said halfheartedly.

Her father summoned up a smile. "You looked very pretty tonight, Ellen. Your mom and I are so proud of you."

A lump rose in Ellen's throat. "Thanks, Daddy."

Mr. Ming pushed open the door. "Tomorrow we'll talk, I promise."

"Okay. Good night." Ellen ran up the stairs quickly, her black-and-gold silk dress rustling. She thought about what he had said as she got ready for bed. Another "discussion" with Mom. What did it mean?

She was almost asleep when she heard their voices. They weren't loud, but somehow she could tell they were emotional. Ellen sat up in bed, her heart pounding. She prayed they'd stop, but the voices still came through the wall, low and intense. She thought she heard her mother crying.

"Ellen?" Her door was pushed open softly, and her younger sister, Suzanne, peeked around it. Her delicate mouth was curved into a frown. "They're arguing again."

"I know. Come on in with me. It's cold."

Suzanne padded over and climbed in next to Ellen. She shivered and pulled the blanket up to her chin. "I hate this so much," she whispered.

"So do I," Ellen said. "I'm going to talk to Dad tomorrow. We have to find out what's going on."

"What if he says they're getting divorced?" Suzanne asked, her dark eyes wide with fear.

Her fourteen-year-old sister was especially sensitive, Ellen knew. Her first year of high school was hard enough, and now she had to deal with all of this, too.

"I don't think he will," Ellen said reassuringly. But she only said it to make Suzanne feel better.

"What will we do if he does?" Suzanne whispered, tears welling up in her eyes.

Just the thought of their parents splitting up was unbearable. Ellen couldn't think of a single encouraging thing to say to her sister. She leaned back against the pillows and turned her face to the wall.

"I don't know," Ellen answered truthfully. "I really don't know."

2 

Couples! Everywhere Brittany Tate looked, she saw nothing but couples. When she got off the school bus that morning, blinded by the bright sun on the snow, she almost crashed into Mark Giordano and Chris Martinez, king and queen of the jocks. They had paused to kiss. Nikki Masters, the golden girl, was just pulling into a parking space with that adorable Niles Butler. From across the quad, loudmouth Robin Fisher, who was with her boyfriend, Calvin Roth, waved to Nikki and Niles.

Brittany pressed her lips together as she headed up the walk. Robin had really spoiled things for her at the Winter Carnival Ball Saturday night. She'd let Brittany have it for setting up a fight between Lacey and Rick. Robin had actually blamed Brittany for Rick's accident! It was bad enough that Brittany herself had felt guilty for her part in the couple's fight. She didn't need Robin to rub it in. And she certainly didn't need Tim Cooper to hear about it!

He'd been standing in the shadows, listening to every word. The rest of the night had been a disaster. Tim had been icily polite, but it was obvious he wished he were a million miles away. And he'd dumped Brittany off on her doorstep like a pile of old laundry.

She had come so close to having Tim for her steady. She'd turned over a new leaf, and her goody-goody act had seemed to work for a while. She'd been incredibly nice, and Tim had finally responded. She should have been swinging hands with him while they walked to school, just like drippy Karen Jacobs and Ben Newhouse, who were solidly back together again. But now Tim thought she was a double-dealing snake. Brittany was conspicuously alone. She seemed like the only girl at River Heights High without a boyfriend!

She'd never forgive Robin Fisher. Never. Brittany gave Robin her trademark drop-dead look as she walked by. Robin merely grinned back at her. Brittany tossed her gleaming dark hair and hurried over to Kim Bishop and Samantha Daley, her best friends. They were in their usual spot, standing near the marble steps of River Heights High North.

"What's going on with you and Robin?" Kim asked, puffs of warm breath hanging in the cold air and accenting her words. Her keen blue eyes shone with the promise of good gossip. "I saw that look you gave her."

Brittany shrugged. "That girl should get a life. She didn't like the fact that I went to the ball with her best friend's ex-boyfriend." Nobody could find out that Robin had yelled at her. She didn't want the whole school to think she'd been the cause of Rick's accident.

Samantha Daley leaned closer, her cinnamon eyes sparkling. "What *did* happen with you and Tim Saturday night?" she asked in her soft southern drawl. "I was too busy having fun to notice."

Kim and Samantha stared at her expectantly. Brittany thought fast. She leaned over and said in a whisper, "I'll tell you a secret. That hunk Tim Cooper is just the teeniest bit boring. Nikki can have him." Brittany shook back her thick, dark hair and laughed. "I'm looking for someone a little wild now."

Normally that comment would impress Samantha and Kim. They'd demand more details, wondering what she was planning. Brittany would be vague and hint at plans she wasn't prepared to reveal. But right then Samantha and Kim were barely listening to her. They were staring over her head.

"Here come the guys," Kim said.

Brittany turned around. Jeremy Pratt and Kyle Kirkwood, Kim and Samantha's boyfriends, were heading for them. Kyle's face brightened at the sight of Sam. Brittany wanted to throw up.

"Hello, gorgeous," Jeremy said to Kim. She smiled regally. The two of them were such a pain, Brittany thought impatiently. They thought they were the hottest thing to hit River Heights High since Mexican Day in the cafeteria.

"We were just talking about the country club dance this weekend," Jeremy said. "It's going to be major."

"And right after the Winter Carnival Ball," Kim said with a sigh. "I'm going to be dead next week."

"It sounds okay," Kyle said, slipping his hands into his pockets to warm them. "I'm not a big fan of the country club, but Samantha really wants to go."

"I can't wait," Samantha said. She slipped her hand into Kyle's.

Brittany tuned out the disgusting display. She was glad to be reminded of the country club dance. It would be the first major function she'd attend as a member. After working her feet off at greasy Slim and Shorty's Cafe to raise the money for her club dues, Brittany decided right then it was time to make all that hard work pay off. And it was time, Brittany decided, for her to be back on top. That meant snaring a fantastic new boyfriend.

"Who's going?" she asked Jeremy.

"Oh, the usual country club crowd," Jeremy said, waving a hand. "No one you'd know."

Brittany's hands tightened on her books. Jeremy was so slimy he must have crawled out of a swamp. He never let her forget that she had only recently become a member—and only a junior member, at that.

"Some of the college crowd will probably be there," Kim added

Brittany sighed. "I'm sick of the college crowd," she said. "Jack Reilly called the other night, but I refused to speak to him."

Brittany had dated Jack for a while, but he had been the one to break things off. There was no way she'd ever give *him* the time of day again.

"You turned down Jack Reilly?" Samantha asked enviously. Kyle frowned.

Brittany waved a careless hand. "Ancient history. Who else is going, Kim?"

"The snobs from Talbot and Fox Hill, of course," Kim replied. Talbot and Fox Hill were the boys' and girls' private schools in River Heights.

"I just hope Chip Worthington isn't there," Jeremy muttered.

Brittany stifled a grin. Kim had told her that Chip had nearly rearranged the aristocratic Pratt profile after a poker game a while ago. She could understand why Jeremy wouldn't want to see him again.

"You could always hire a bodyguard, Jeremy," she said sweetly. Kim smiled, but quickly turned it into a frown when Jeremy shot her a nasty look.

"It's not that I'm afraid of him," Jeremy returned quickly. "He makes all these comments about Kim just to give me grief. He keeps leering at her and saying things like, 'What are you doing with the most beautiful girl in River Heights, Pratt?' Stuff like that. It's totally annoying."

"Really," Kim agreed, tossing her shiny blond hair.

Jeremy might hate it, but Kim wasn't too upset, Brittany was sure. Who wouldn't like being called the most beautiful girl in River Heights? Of course, Chip Worthington hadn't met Brittany Tate yet.

Then it hit her. Why not go after Chip Worthington? His family was better connected than even the Pratts! They'd practically founded River Heights. Brittany was bored with all the boys at school. Why not stake out some new territory? Let Kim and Jeremy be king and queen of River Heights High. Brittany and Chip would run the town!

"You should have seen the look Brittany just gave Robin," Calvin Roth said, laughing. "It could have peeled paint." Robin had just finished telling Nikki, Niles, and Lacey how she had yelled at Brittany at the Winter Carnival Ball.

"I've gotten that drop-dead look a few times," Nikki admitted, stomping her feet to get them warm.

"How was I supposed to know Tim was eavesdropping Saturday night?" Robin said. "But don't ask me if I feel sorry about it."

"Well, I just want to put it all behind me," Lacey said decidedly. She looked like a new person. Her skin was glowing, and her pale blue eyes were shining. Even her hair seemed more lustrous. It was as though she'd come back to life over the weekend.

"So Rick wasn't angry at you at all?" Robin asked. "He didn't blame you for the accident?"

"Not one bit," Lacey said. "We had a long talk about it on Sunday. He said it was his fault. He'd just been upset about his grades, and he felt like everyone was on his case. So he overreacted to my asking him about the cheating ring. He said he should have known better than to go climbing right after that."

"So he didn't tell you that he doesn't want to see you anymore?" Robin asked.

"No," Lacey said, her smile widening. She knew what Robin was getting at.

"So he still loves you, then," Robin continued.

Lacey nodded. "Oh, yes."

Robin put a finger to her forehead. She looked at Nikki. "Now, who told Lacey all those things would happen?"

Nikki grinned. "They must have been a couple of very smart people," she said.

"Hmmm. They must have been some very good friends," Robin said. "I wonder—"

"All right, you guys," Lacey broke in, laughing. "I surrender. I know you told me all that a thousand times. I should have listened. I guess I needed to hear it from Rick. But you can say I told you so, if you want to be mean and rub it in."

"I told you so," Nikki and Robin said together, and the three friends burst out laughing.

"Well, I'm glad Rick is better," Niles said. "I was just getting to know him, when he fell on his head. I call that very inconsiderate."

"He can receive more visitors in a couple of days," Lacey said happily.

"Great!" Robin said. "We'll go cheer him up."

"When do you think you'll be able to go back to your old schedule, Lacey?" Nikki asked.

"Not for a few weeks, at least," Lacey said, "I want to spend as much time as I can with Rick now that he's awake. He needs me more than ever. How are you doing at Platters, Robin?"

Robin grinned, her nose pink from the cold. "I haven't been fired yet. I think

Lenny might even be getting used to me." Robin was way over her head working Lacey's job at the record store, but until Lacey could come back, she'd stick it out, no matter what.

"And Ellen says she can go on handling my class secretary responsibilities," Lacey went on. "She actually wants to, as a matter of fact."

"Every time I see Ellen these days, she's rushing to some meeting," Nikki said thoughtfully. "She's always been pretty involved in school activities, but now I think she's on every committee there is."

"You guys should hear her latest idea," Calvin said. "I was just talking to her before Robin got here. She's on her way to ask Ben Newhouse about a roast pig and sunglasses."

Lacey, Nikki, Niles, and Robin exchanged glances.

"Okay, Cal, what are you talking about?" Robin demanded. "Let us in on it. What's the next big event at River Heights High?"

Across the quad, Ben was frowning down at Ellen. "A *luau?*" he asked.

"I thought we'd call it something like

Maui Madness," Ellen said. "We could have it on a Friday night, and everyone could wear Hawaiian shirts and sunglasses to school that day to get in the mood. We could put sand on the floor of the gym, and—"

"The coaches would flip," Karen Jacobs said, brushing back her light brown hair. "They'd never let you do that."

Ellen frowned. Then she snapped her fingers. "I know! We could begin the party at the pool. Then we'd move to the gym for refreshments and dancing."

"Coach Dixon would *really* flip at that," Karen said. Coach Dixon was the swim-team coach.

"We could have pineapple chicken-fingers and tropical punch," Ellen went on. She turned back to Ben. "We have all those palm trees Sasha and her committee made just sitting in the art department closet."

"I thought we wouldn't get snow for the Winter Carnival," Ben said defensively. "We had to come up with a new theme. Thank heaven Sasha talked me out of the tropical theme in time."

"It was a terrific idea!" Ellen said soothingly. "That's why we should still do it."

Ben sighed. "I guess we could. But I'm exhausted after Winter Carnival. I couldn't organize another committee."

"I'll do it," Ellen said. "I've already made a couple of calls. I just need your help, that's all."

"But, Ellen," Karen protested, "you're already working on the Clean Up Your School committee, not to mention being treasurer and interim secretary of the class."

"I have time," Ellen assured them. She would make time. This project could fill up a lot of empty hours.

"There's another problem," Ben said. "As the class treasurer, you must know what it is. I don't think we have enough money to do it."

"I already figured that out, too," Ellen said. "We could have a used record and tape sale. Everybody could donate tapes and records they're tired of. Then the committee would price them, and we'd have a sale."

The bell rang, and all the kids stomped snow off their boots and gratefully headed for the warmth the building promised.

"Sounds good," Ben said.

Ellen grinned. "I knew I could count on

you guys." She said goodbye to Ben and Karen and hurried along the shoveled walkway. Another project to fill her time was what she needed. But how long could planning a school dance cover up the awful fears inside of her?

3

Tuesday morning the girls and Mrs. Ming were eating breakfast alone. Mr. Ming had left for work before they were awake, and Mrs. Ming had been silent and distracted while she drank her coffee. Her mood spread, and Ellen and Suzanne were quiet, too, as they poured their cereal and juice.

"I have to get to work, girls," she said. "Oh, I almost forgot." She glanced down at a note she had written to herself. "Your father and I have an appointment this afternoon around four. We'll bring dinner home with us. Is there anything special you'd like?"

Normally Ellen and Suzanne would have been in heaven. They loved to eat take-out food and would argue over the merits of pizza, deli, or food at the new Thai restaurant in town. But now they both shook their heads.

"Whatever you want, Mom," Ellen said.

"I don't care," Suzanne mumbled.

Mrs. Ming pushed a hand through her short, dark hair. "Okay. Have a good day at school, and I'll see you tonight." Mrs. Ming managed an exclusive clothing store downtown. She was wearing an elegant gray suit and matching suede shoes, and a dramatic silver pin was on one shoulder. To anyone else, she'd seem impeccably dressed, but Ellen knew her mother well. Her mom had skipped lipstick and earrings, and that was a tip-off to Ellen that her usually meticulous mother was upset.

"Have a good day, too, Mom," she said.

Mrs. Ming nodded, but it was as though she hadn't heard Ellen. She walked out of the kitchen quickly, forgetting the note she had intended to take with her.

Ellen turned back to the table and her cereal, but she wasn't hungry. She looked over at Suzanne, who was staring at the note Mrs. Ming had left. Suzanne looked up with worried eyes.

"What is it?" Ellen asked, alarmed.

Suzanne pushed the note toward her. "Look who Mom and Dad have an appointment with," she said.

Ellen looked at the pad. "Sachs, Tobin, and Downing," her mother had written. "211 Willow Street." Ellen recognized the name immediately. Everett Sachs was the Mings' lawyer.

Suzanne's spoon clattered into her empty bowl. Her lips trembled. "Now we know for sure," she said to Ellen. Her voice was thick with unshed tears. "Mom and Dad are getting a divorce!"

After school on Tuesday, Brittany had to work at Blooms, her mother's florist shop at the mall. But she promised to meet Kim and Samantha for a snack at a pizza place.

Her mother had her unpack about a million boxes of tulips, so Brittany was late when she finally pushed through the crowd to Kim and Samantha's booth. They were sitting, surrounded by packages.

"Here, let me move these," Kim said, taking a shopping bag and dumping it on the floor. "We did some major shopping damage today."

"I can see that," Brittany said shortly. She was burning with jealousy. She'd depleted all her savings to pay her membership dues at the club, and she had no money left for clothes. It was so frustrating! She didn't have enough saved from her job at Blooms to buy more than a new pair of socks.

"Have some pizza," Samantha urged. She pushed an empty paper plate toward Brittany and indicated the piping hot pie in the middle of the table. "I almost didn't get to buy a new dress for the country club dance," she said. "Can you believe it? I almost died when my father said no. But I cried and cried, and he just melted. I am *so* glad—the dress is incredible."

"It's hot," Kim said. "I mean the dress, not the pizza. Samantha, you're going to knock Kyle's eyes out."

"And what about you, Tate?" Samantha said to Brittany. "Kim snagged the best dress at Glad Rags. It's gorgeous."

"Terrific," Brittany said. She folded her pizza slice expertly and took a bite. The last thing in the world she needed right now was to hear about Kim's new dress!

"You should definitely run over there this afternoon," Kim went on, delicately cutting her slice with a knife and fork. Where did she think she was, Le St. Tropez? Brittany thought sourly as Kim put a tiny piece of pizza in her mouth.

"You'll want to buy something before everything's gone," Samantha advised.

Sometimes Kim and Samantha could be

so insensitive, Brittany fumed. Just last week she'd told both of them that her mother had put her foot down and said that her ruby velvet dress was the last new dress she could have for the season, unless she paid for one herself. Kim had looked horrified. The concept of a limited clothing allowance was worse than the thought of Jeremy's Porsche breaking down again. Samantha had just looked bored. Didn't they remember that Brittany couldn't buy a new dress?

"I'll see," Brittany mumbled.

"Plus, it's your first big event as a member," Kim said. "You'll want to look absolutely fabulous."

She *did* want to look absolutely fabulous. "I might wear my black strapless minidress," she said.

Kim looked unimpressed. "Well, you always look nice in that," she said vaguely.

Brittany flushed with embarrassment. Kim didn't have to rub it in! She looked away to hide her flaming cheeks and caught sight of Robin sitting with Nikki and Lacey. Robin was wearing a bright gold blazer that Brittany had seen her wear plenty of times before. But that day Robin had gathered the material in the back and placed a clunky costume-jewelry pin there to hold the pleats together. She had wound a deep purple scarf several times around her neck. Brittany had to admit the effect was fantastic.

She couldn't stand the girl, but Brittany did admire her fashion sense and wished she had a friend like Robin. She didn't buy many new things, but with a scarf or the right jewelry she could make her old things look new.

But Brittany was stuck with two friends who didn't understand how awful it was not to be able to buy a new dress whenever you wanted. And they would babble on about their new clothes without thinking of her at all.

It just wasn't fair. Brittany pushed her pizza away and wiped her mouth with her napkin. Secretly, she made a resolution. She'd have a new knockout dress to wear Saturday night—no matter what she had to do to get it!

After school Ellen helped to letter posters for the Clean Up Your School campaign. She discussed a possible recycling plan with Cheryl Worth, the president of the student council. And she nailed down the plans for the record and tape sale, then cleared the details with Ms. Rose, the faculty advisor for the student council.

Everything was all set for the sale, which would begin on Friday.

But finally Ellen had to go home. It was almost six when she put her key in the door. Her parents' car wasn't in the driveway, so she knew they weren't home yet. The first floor was dark. Ellen stood a moment, listening to the silence. Usually the house was lively at six o'clock. Suzanne would be practicing the piano, and her mother would be getting dinner ready with her father. He'd be home from his job at his accounting firm, and he'd be chopping vegetables and exchanging stories with Mrs. Ming about their days. Maybe her parents would be having a glass of wine together. Ellen would hear them laughing all the way in the family room.

Ellen shook her head. She wouldn't cry. Once she started, she wouldn't be able to stop. She slowly climbed the stairs, wondering where Suzanne was. She didn't see a light coming from under her closed bedroom door at the top of the stairs. Ellen hesitated in the hall. And then she heard a sound. Suzanne was crying.

Ellen pushed open the door. Suzanne was lying curled up on top of her bedspread, a wet tissue clutched in her fist. Her long black hair was falling out of its ponytail, and her skin looked red and blotchy. She must have been crying for some time, Ellen realized.

"Suzanne, don't cry," she said gently, going over and sitting next to her on the bed. Ellen smoothed her hair. Suzanne had the sensitivity that went along with talent. She was a genius on the piano and wanted to be a concert pianist. She'd already appeared in numerous recitals, and her steely nerves always impressed Ellen.

But when it came to her social life, Suzanne was nervous and uncertain. It was hard for her to make friends, and now that she was in high school, it was even more difficult. She just wasn't interested in boys and clothes, the way other freshman girls were. Her life revolved around her music and her family. Poor Suzanne, Ellen thought. Whatever happened would be hardest on her.

"I can't help it," Suzanne said, her voice muffled against her wet pillow. "My life is so awful. I hate school. I have no friends. And now I just know Daddy will be moving out. Everybody's parents get divorced sooner or later."

"That's not true and you know it," Ellen said soothingly. "And we don't know anything for sure yet."

Suzanne sat up and wiped her eyes. "It's

not knowing that's so hard," she said. "I keep imagining the worst."

Just then they heard the front door open and close downstairs.

"Anybody home?" Mrs. Ming called.

Ellen ran to the top of the stairs. "We're up here," she said.

"Well, come on down," Mrs. Ming said. She looked strained and tired as she took off her heavy winter coat. "Daddy and I picked up some food, and we should eat it while it's hot. He's in the kitchen."

"Be right down," Ellen agreed.

She went back to Suzanne's room. "You'd better wash your face," she advised. "And I promise that after dinner I'll ask Mom and Dad what's going on. Okay?"

"Okay," Suzanne agreed nervously.

Ellen waited for Suzanne at the top of the stairs, and they went down together. Mr. and Mrs. Ming were unpacking the food and dishing it onto plates.

"Mexican," her father said as the girls walked in. He was trying to sound hearty, but he couldn't pull it off. "Tacos, enchiladas, refried beans, the works. And I got the hottest taco sauce to go with it, just for you, Ellen."

Ellen tried to smile. She loved Mexican food. But that night it was torture to crunch through her taco, and her enchilada tasted like dust. Her parents barely ate anything, and nobody said a word. There was only an occasional "Please pass the guacamole."

When they were finally through, Ellen pushed aside her half-eaten enchilada and gathered her courage. She caught Suzanne's eye across the table and nodded. It was time.

But before she could say anything, her father cleared his throat nervously. He loosened his tie with quick, sensitive fingers. "Your mother and I thought it was time for a family conference," he said.

Ellen and Suzanne exchanged frightened looks. They were finally going to hear the bad news.

Her father hesitated, and Suzanne suddenly banged her soda can on the table. "Go ahead," she said shrilly. "Tell us. You're sorry, but you're getting a divorce."

Her mother and father exchanged puzzled glances. Then Mrs. Ming rushed in quickly to reassure Suzanne. "No, no, sweetie. Your father and I are fine. That is, our marriage is fine." She looked helplessly at her husband. "You'd better tell them, David."

Mr. Ming looked at his daughters. "I love

you both very much," he said quietly. "And that's the reason I haven't told you this news yet. But it might be in the papers soon, and I have to tell you now. I'm in serious trouble. I might even have to go to jail!"

4

"Jail?" Ellen blurted. "What do you mean, Daddy?"

Suzanne said nothing. Her small face looked white and pinched.

"I'm being accused of embezzling by a Mr. Bishop, one of my clients," Mr. Ming said slowly. "There's some money missing. I didn't take it, but it looks to the client as though I did."

"But you're innocent," Ellen protested. Her stomach felt tied in knots. How could this be happening to her father? He was so honest, so good. "They'll find out that you didn't take the money."

"That's what I've been telling myself," Mr. Ming said. "But all the evidence points to me, I'm afraid. Your mom and I went to see our lawyer this afternoon. So far, Mr. Bishop is only bringing civil charges against me. But we heard today that his lawyer is threatening to go to the state attorney and demand an investigation. That means criminal charges could be filed. And that means a trial, and possibly jail if I'm convicted."

Ellen couldn't believe this was happening. Through her confusion, a name floated in front of her. "Mr. Bishop?" she croaked. *"Kim Bishop's father?"*

Her mother nodded. "You know how influential he is. Even though he's not rich, he's got a very good, very classy lawyer. He's determined to press any charges that he can because he believes Daddy's guilty."

Mrs. Ming stopped talking, and Ellen couldn't meet her parents' eyes. She only stared at her half-empty plate. She couldn't seem to absorb what was going on. Next to her, Suzanne had started to cry silently.

"I'm sorry this has happened," Mr. Ming said. "Once this gets out, it might be pretty hard on you girls. If the news isn't in the paper tomorrow, it will be on Thursday or Friday."

"Maybe it will be a small mention," Mrs. Ming said. "The kids at school might never find out."

Ellen hadn't even thought about what would happen at school. Now her heart started to beat fast at the thought of the stares and whispers. Surely Kim Bishop knew the story. Would she be kind and keep it to herself? Ellen didn't really know Kim, but she knew she wasn't the nicest person in town. Someone like Nikki or Karen would keep the secret. But Kim . . .

Then Ellen looked over at her parents. She saw that they were holding hands. Their fingers were gripping each other's tightly. She could see that her mother was fighting not to cry. It must have been very hard for them to tell her and Suzanne.

Love washed over Ellen, and tears stung her eyes. She didn't care about school just then. She only cared that her parents were hurting so much. She stood up and went to her father. She bent over and hugged him tightly.

"It's okay, Daddy. I love you," she whispered.

Suzanne stood up and ran over, too. The four of them hugged one another awkwardly. They were a family. They would stick together, no matter what was ahead.

Brittany slammed her bedroom door shut and stomped over to her bed. She threw herself on it and punched her pillow angrily. Her mother was so mean! She absolutely refused to give Brittany an advance on her salary at Blooms. The flower shop couldn't afford it, she said, and she didn't intend to spoil Brittany. She'd just have to wear one of the many pretty dresses already hanging in her closet.

It wasn't fair! How could she snare Chip Worthington or *anybody* in an old rag?

Her phone rang, and Brittany glared at it. It was probably Kim or Samantha calling to tell her more details of their fabulous new dresses. Brittany finally snatched up the phone. "Hello?"

"Brittany, I've got news."

It was Kim. Brittany sighed and cradled the receiver against her ear as she reached for a fashion magazine to leaf through while Kim talked. Brittany was probably in for at least twenty minutes of gush about Jeremy Pratt.

"What is it, Kim? Something up with Jeremy?"

"No, this is really major. My dad just

told me. He uses Ellen Ming's father's accounting firm for his business, you know?"

"No, I didn't," Brittany said, bored. She turned to the section "Dazzling Dresses for Evening."

"Well," Kim said in a low, thrilled voice, "my father just told me that he's filing charges against Mr. Ming for embezzlement! There's all this money missing, and Mr. Ming stole it."

Brittany pushed the magazine aside. "Is your father sure?"

"Of course he's sure. He said Mr. Ming is guilty as sin. You can't argue with the facts."

"Wow," Brittany said. "This *is* big." She felt a brief flash of compassion for Ellen. Imagine having a criminal for a father! Maybe it wasn't so bad having a nobody for a father after all.

"I think it's just awful," Kim said. "My poor father is so upset. I'm sure the school will be in an uproar about this."

"What do you mean, Kim?" Brittany asked. Suddenly she felt nervous. Sometimes Kim could really go overboard. "You're not going to tell people at school about this, are you?" she asked.

"Of course I am," Kim said promptly. "Why shouldn't I? I'm going to call

Jeremy and Samantha right after this. I think everyone has a right to know, don't you?"

"I don't know," Brittany said slowly. "It's not like Mr. Ming has been convicted yet. And it could be really tough on Ellen. I think you should wait on this, Kim."

"Since when did you develop scruples?" Kim asked scornfully. "Or is this still your goody-goody act? I can't keep track of all your personality changes, Brittany."

Brittany bit back a sharp retort. She wasn't being a prude, but even *she* had limits. "Listen, Kim," she said carefully, "this is serious stuff you're talking about. Maybe you should wait until you have all the facts." Maybe she *had* changed a little bit, Brittany thought. She knew after Rick's accident that casual gossip could be truly hurtful sometimes.

Kim wasn't fazed by Brittany's advice. "I *do* have the facts," she said flatly. "My father told me everything. Look, it'll probably be in the paper tomorrow, anyway, so I don't know why we're arguing. See you, Brittany." There was a sharp click as Kim hung up.

Slowly Brittany replaced the receiver. She didn't even know Ellen that well, so why did she feel so sorry for her? All Brittany knew was, if Kim didn't reconsider, Ellen could be in for a very rough time.

As soon as she was dressed Wednesday morning, Ellen rushed downstairs. The morning paper was lying on the kitchen table, and she grabbed it and went through it quickly. She didn't see any mention of her father. Ellen went back to the front page and started over, just to make sure.

"There's nothing in the paper," her mother said, coming into the kitchen. "Thank goodness. But there's still the evening edition." She paused by Ellen's chair and gently stroked her hair. "Are you okay, honey?"

Ellen gave a wobbly smile. "I'm okay, Mom."

"Probably the kids at school won't know anything about it," Mrs. Ming said, trying to reassure her.

Ellen sighed. "Oh, Mom, Mr. Bishop's daughter is the biggest gossip in school," she told her.

"Oh," Mrs. Ming said quietly. Then she took a deep breath. "I'm going to give you and Suzanne a ride to school today. Is Suzie dressed yet?"

"I think so," Ellen answered. "But, Mom, won't you be late for work?"

Mrs. Ming straightened a snowy white cuff on her black wool dress. "The shop can open fifteen minutes late today," she said. "Now, I baked some blueberry muffins this morning. They're on the counter. Where is Suzanne? I'd better hurry her along."

Mrs. Ming's high heels tapped out of the kitchen. Ellen went to get a muffin. She knew her mother was trying to make things easier for her and Suzanne. She didn't want them to have to face the school bus. But what was the use of postponing disaster? Ellen wondered as she poured her orange juice. They'd have to face the kids at school eventually.

Later the three of them rode to River Heights High in silence. Ellen's stomach was in knots, and she knew Suzanne's was, too. Her little sister just stared numbly out the window.

Her mother pulled her Saab into the school parking lot. "Okay, kids," she said brightly. "Here we are." There was a fixed smile on Mrs. Ming's face. But as she watched Ellen and Suzanne stare, unmoving, out at the snowy quad, her smile faltered and she gripped the steering wheel tighter. "Go on," she said softly. "Remember that your father is innocent, no matter what anyone says. Hold your heads up and be as strong as you can."

Ellen and Suzanne scrambled out of the car and started up a shoveled-out path to the school. Suddenly the distance from the car to school seemed miles long. Ellen saw heads turning toward them and mouths moving rapidly. Up by the marble steps, Kim leaned over and whispered to Jeremy Pratt, who stood looking down his nose, unblinking, at the two sisters.

Suzanne's footsteps lagged just then. "Come on, Suzanne," Ellen urged. "Remember what Mom said. I'll walk you to your homeroom, if you want." Ellen would do anything to protect her sister. But who would protect Ellen?

Ben Newhouse and Karen Jacobs broke away from a knot of students and turned in Ellen's direction. Karen's cheeks were flushed from the cold, and her chin was held high as she made her way toward Ellen. Ben's eyebrows were knitted together in a frown. Ellen felt afraid. What would they say to her?

"Ellen!" Karen said in a loud voice. "We've been waiting for you. We've got so much to discuss about the luau."

"Have you come up with any more fabulous ideas?" Ben asked. The two of them swung into step with Ellen and Suzanne.

"That's a cute hat and scarf set, Suzanne," Karen said. "Where did you get it?"

Ellen's throat felt tight as she continued moving toward the school. Karen had gently engaged shy Suzanne in conversation, and Ellen felt very grateful to both of her friends.

"Hi, Ellen," Nikki Masters called from a little cleared circle off to Ellen's right. Robin Fisher waved from there, too, as Lacey Dupree ran over.

"I want to talk to you during lunch," Lacey said. "I want you to keep me up on our junior-class projects."

"Sure," Ellen said dazedly. Nikki and Niles Butler and Robin and Calvin Roth came over to walk with them, too. Ellen was surrounded by friends as she reached the marble steps. Kim was opening her mouth to say something when Brittany Tate spoke out in a loud voice.

"I've got a great idea. Let's shock our homeroom teachers and be on time for a change."

Relief flooded through Ellen as she stomped the snow off her boots. Kim had been about to say something mean, that was obvious. Ellen didn't know why Brittany had just prevented it, but she didn't care. Sometimes support could come from the most unlikely places.

At lunch Brittany sat alone at a table, working on her column, "Off the Record." People stopped by to chat, but she always pointed to her notebook and pleaded a deadline. She didn't mind eating alone, as long as it was obvious that she was working.

Her deadline really wasn't until the next week, but Brittany knew DeeDee Smith, the editor in chief of the *Record,* wasn't pleased that she always handed her column in at the last minute. The editor in chief was very businesslike and dedicated, but Brittany was dedicated, too. She was going to be editor in chief next year—that is, she hoped to be. She *had* to be.

Kim and Jeremy were late. That was a treat. Brittany took a bite of her tuna sandwich. She and Kim were close, but ever since Jeremy came on the scene, all the things that annoyed her about Kim seemed to get worse. Kim was even more snobby, more insensitive, and made more cutting remarks than ever before. She'd proved it that very day by spreading the story of Ellen's father all over the school.

Just then Kim and Jeremy swept into

the cafeteria, holding hands. They looked as though they expected everyone to get up and applaud, Brittany thought, and laughed to herself. She bent over her notebook again.

Kim came up a minute later. "Where's Samantha?" she asked, dumping her books on the table.

"She eats at Kyle's table today, remember?" Brittany prodded.

"Oh, right." Kim snickered. "I think it's the most infantile system—it makes me dizzy. One day Kyle eats with us, then the next day Samantha eats with the brain crowd. Then they have a day just to sit with their friends. Poor Sam. I wonder what she talks about with his crowd. Logarithms?"

"She looks pretty bored," Brittany agreed. "I wonder how long this will last."

"I give her a week," Jeremy pronounced. "Then she'll be back here where the action is."

"Working on your column?" Kim asked as she took a yogurt and a banana out of her purse.

"It's next week's," Brittany told her.

Jeremy peeked over her shoulder at Brittany's notes as he headed for the seat next to Kim. Annoyed, Brittany shielded her work.

"Oh, excuse me," Jeremy said. "Top secret, huh?"

"You'll see my column when the *Record* comes out, like everyone else," Brittany said. "I don't give sneak previews."

Kim stirred her yogurt. "Well, at least you have a great topic."

"Yeah," Brittany agreed. "Everyone will want to know what I thought of Winter Carnival."

Kim shook her head. "I wasn't talking about that. I mean Ellen Ming. Of course you're going to cover that in your column."

Brittany stirred uneasily. She didn't want to mention the Ming family troubles in her column. It wasn't really appropriate, and it seemed pretty mean, too. She wished that Kim would keep her nose out of it. "Well, I'm not," she said. "It has nothing to do with the school."

"Of course it does," Kim said indignantly. "Haven't you heard the latest? Ellen is organizing a record sale to make money for the luau. For the rest of the week, we're supposed to bring in records and tapes that we don't want anymore. Then Ellen's committee will price them and hold a sale in the gym after school on Friday and on Monday at lunchtime."

"So?" Brittany said irritably. "That sounds like a good idea to raise money."

"Sure," Jeremy put in. "But let's hope the money that gets raised goes toward the luau."

"And *not* in Ellen Ming's pocket," Kim said smugly. "Somebody ought to supervise that girl. I think it's ridiculous that the daughter of a criminal is in charge of the junior-class funds." Kim pointed her spoon at Brittany. "And *that's* a feature story if you ask me."

Brittany bent over her pad again. Kim and Jeremy might have a point. That story could cause a sensation at school. Brittany frowned. What was more important—protecting Ellen, or becoming editor in chief next year?

5

On Thursday Karen and Ben were waiting for Ellen in front of school again. Ellen was relieved that the record and tape sale was the next day. She had a million details to attend to, and she would have to stay late that day to help price the records and tapes people brought in.

All day Ellen tried her best to ignore the stares and whispers. The hardest thing was to keep her head up and walk normally. All Ellen wanted to do was scurry through the halls with her head down. Once she was in a class, she felt safe. It was the hallways and cafeteria that scared her, just waiting for someone to make a crack about her father. But everyone just talked behind her back or whispered as she went by. All except for Kim Bishop.

"I don't know how she even dares to come to school at all," she said loudly to Samantha as Ellen passed by them to enter the cafeteria at lunch.

Ellen headed toward Karen and Ben's table, her cheeks on fire. Her knees were shaking as she sank into a chair.

"I saw Kim Bishop say something as you went by," Karen said sympathetically. "Are you okay?"

"I'm okay," Ellen said, swallowing hard.

Ben slammed his hand down on the table. His usually mild brown eyes were furious. "Kim should be locked up!" he exclaimed. Karen elbowed him sharply in the side, and he blushed. "I—I didn't mean that, Ellen. I mean—"

Ellen gave a tiny smile. "It's okay, Ben. Do you think jail hasn't been on my mind?"

Karen frowned. "You think your father might go to jail?"

"It's possible," Ellen admitted. "I might be a pessimist, but I don't think many people besides me, my mom, and Suzanne think he's innocent."

"I do," Karen said firmly.

"I do, too," Ben agreed.

"Thanks, you guys," Ellen said around a lump in her throat. "That means a lot."

"Look," Ben said briskly. "They can't prove your father took that money, and they don't jail people without sufficient evidence. No one goes to jail while there's reasonable doubt about his innocence. That's what our justice system is all about."

"I keep telling myself that," Ellen said. She smiled wryly. "I just hope people like Kim Bishop aren't on the jury."

After the last bell, Ellen walked to the student council meeting. The council met every two weeks with all of the class officers. She took her usual seat next to Martin Salko, the vice-president of the junior class, and waited for Ms. Rose, the student council faculty advisor, to show up. While she waited, Ellen began to feel uneasy. Usually, they'd all be laughing and joking with one another until the stern Ms. Rose made her appearance. She was a no-nonsense person, and the time for any fun had to come before the meeting started. But that day people seemed oddly quiet.

Ellen saw Juliann Wade, the treasurer of the student council, whisper something to

Patty Casey, who was the secretary. They both glanced at Ellen, then quickly looked away. Juliann and Patty always backed each other when the council had to vote or make a decision. Juliann had always acted as if she resented Ellen. Lacey claimed it was because Ellen did more, as treasurer of the junior class, than Juliann did as treasurer of the student council. Ellen wished that Lacey was there for moral support, but Lacey needed to be with Rick even more now that he was conscious.

Ben arrived and took a seat next to Martin Salko. Kevin Hoffman came in and went to sit next to Cheryl Worth, who was president of the council. Kevin grinned warmly at Ellen as he slid into his seat.

Feeling a blush start on her cheeks, Ellen stared down at her pen on the table top. Sometimes the feelings she had when she had her crush on Kevin came back. Nothing had ever come of her silly crush, not even one date. Ellen knew she was too serious for Kevin, who was full of jokes and mischief. Creative and fun, he wrote a humor column for the *Record* and had starred in many school productions. He couldn't be more different from dependable Ellen Ming, with her aptitude for chemistry and math and her organizational skills.

At least Ellen had realized her crush was hopeless within a couple of weeks. She'd managed to forget her interest in Kevin Hoffman—most of the time. Still, there was something about his unruly red-brown hair and easy grin that made her smile.

Ms. Rose walked into the room with her brisk step. "Good afternoon, people. Let's get started," she said. "Patty, will you read the minutes from the last meeting?"

Patty Casey stood and read what they'd discussed at the last meeting, which mostly concerned the Clean Up Your School campaign. When she'd finished, Ms. Rose studied her notes for a minute.

"Today, the first item on the agenda," she said, "is the proposal for a luau. A committee has already been formed, headed by Ellen Ming, and she's submitted a budget to me. I'll pass it around for all of you to see in a moment. Since the committee will be mainly using the decorations from the tropical theme for the Winter Carnival that we scrapped, the cost won't be too high. And the committee has high hopes that the record and tape sales will take care of the rest of the costs. They plan to use taped music at the luau, not a band, and have limited refreshments. Now, Ellen, how's the whole plan going?"

"Fine," Ellen said. "We have volunteers lined up to handle the record and tape sales. After this I'll be going to my committee meeting to price old records people have brought in."

"Sounds great," Kevin Hoffman said. "I hope the art club made enough leis!"

"I've also talked to Mr. Meacham about the day of the luau," Ellen said. "He said we can wear leis and Hawaiian shirts and all that stuff. We just can't wear sunglasses in class," she said with a grin.

"It sounds fine. Keep us posted," Ms. Rose said. She studied her notes again. "Now, if there's nothing else on the luau, let's get to—"

"Ms. Rose?" Juliann Wade waved her hand in the air.

Ms. Rose looked up. "Yes, Juliann?"

"I was wondering who's handling the proceeds from the record and tape sale."

Ms. Rose frowned at Juliann, but she turned to Ellen. "Ellen?"

Ellen saw Patty Casey poke Juliann underneath the table. Her heart began to flutter. "I am," she said in a shaky voice.

"What's your point, Juliann?" Ms. Rose asked frostily. Ellen had a feeling Ms. Rose knew what the girl was getting at—and she didn't like it.

Juliann shook back her blond hair

defiantly. "I'm just wondering if we should reconsider having Ellen handle the funds, that's all. I'd be glad to take over."

"I agree with Juliann," Patty said quickly.

Ms. Rose studied the two girls. Her thin lips pressed together. "And what exactly do you agree with, Patty?"

Patty's eyes traveled around the room as if she was seeking an answer. "Well, that maybe Juliann should take charge of the funds. She *is* school treasurer."

Juliann nodded. "Especially under the circumstances . . ." she said meaningfully, letting her voice trail off.

The room was quiet. Did that mean that people were shocked, or that they agreed with Juliann? Ellen felt sick. She was afraid she would faint, she felt so dizzy. She pushed her thick black bangs off her forehead with a hot hand. How could this be happening? They thought she wasn't trustworthy enough to take charge of the money!

She felt Ben stir next to her, but before he could say anything, Kevin Hoffman spoke up.

"That's very nice of you, Juliann." Kevin's voice was calm, but it held a deadly undertone Ellen had never heard before. "Ellen *has* been doing two jobs since Lacey Dupree has dropped out temporarily. She could feel overloaded. I'm sure those were the circumstances you were talking about, right?"

Juliann swallowed. She glanced at Ms. Rose, who was giving her a cold stare. "Of course," she mumbled.

"But Ellen is doing such a fantastic job as usual," Kevin went on steadily, "that as long as she feels she can handle it, I see no reason to make a change. Do you feel you can handle this on top of Lacey's responsibilities, Ellen?"

Ellen looked at Kevin. His green eyes had a fierce look. He nodded at her, giving her courage. He was on her side! "Yes," she managed to choke out.

"Then let's not waste any more time," Ms. Rose said crisply. "We have more important business—the recycling program that Ellen brought up at the last meeting. It was a brilliant idea, and we need to go over the details. Cheryl, can you give me a summary of what you and Ellen have come up with?"

Everyone in the room relaxed, except for Ellen. Her heart was racing, and she tried to calm herself by studying her clasped hands. Kevin had saved her neck, all right. And he'd done it in the best possible way. He hadn't made the situation worse by yelling at Juliann. He'd acted as if there couldn't possibly be a reason to mistrust Ellen. She'd always be grateful to him for that. But Ellen couldn't get over the fact that Juliann had been so cruel in the first place.

Cheryl's voice faded into the background as Ellen fought back tears. Suddenly she realized that she hadn't thought of the worst thing about her father's situation. He might not go to jail, that was true. But even if he didn't, his life could be destroyed. He would always be under a cloud of suspicion. How could he continue in his accounting firm with that hanging over his head?

Ellen had just seen something she wished she hadn't. People could take a rumor or a suspicion and they could use it to disgrace someone. If Ellen was facing that kind of attitude in a student council meeting, what would her father face at work? Ellen had never realized how cruel people could be. She shivered with foreboding. Things could get a lot worse before they got better.

Brittany listened from her bedroom. She heard her mother's quick footsteps as she prepared dinner in the kitchen. The evening news blared from the TV in the den, where her father was watching it and Tamara was doing her homework. Everyone was busy. It was time.

Her heart began to beat faster. It was the only way, she told herself. How else could she buy a killer dress for the country club dance? She had to take her mother's charge card. She'd done it once before and gotten in major trouble, but this time would be different. By the time her mother got the bill next month, Brittany would have saved enough money from her job at Blooms to pay back the cost of the dress—or most of it, anyway. And if she was grounded for a few days, so what? She'd have a new boyfriend and a whole new life. A couple of days at home wouldn't kill her.

Holding her breath, Brittany inched down the hall. She heard something sizzling in the kitchen. She smelled garlic, and deduced that her mother was stir-frying vegetables in her wok, her newest kitchen toy. Good. The noise of the frying should cover Brittany's footsteps.

Her mother's purse was lying right on the table next to the hall closet. Brittany walked silently in her stocking feet, pausing every few seconds to listen carefully. All she could hear was the sizzling of oil and the blare of the TV.

She reached her mother's huge purse

and began to go through it. Her mother treated the purse as a briefcase, and it was crammed with items. A paperback book, a wool scarf, gloves, appointment book . . . Brittany bit her lip as she went through it. Where was her wallet?

Finally her fingers found the leather billfold. Brittany's fingers were shaking as she extracted the credit card from the side pocket holder. She hoped her mother didn't decide to splurge on something at the mall the next morning. Friday afternoon, Brittany was scheduled to work at Blooms. It would be easy to replace the card then—after she'd made a quick trip to Glad Rags.

Her heartbeat was slowing back to normal as she closed the flap on the purse. She turned around and almost fainted.

Her mother was leaning against the wall in her apron, tapping a wooden spoon against her palm. "Did you find what you wanted, Brittany?" she asked.

6

Brittany thought fast. Her mother might not have actually seen her take the credit card. "I was just looking for—a tissue," she said quickly. It sounded pretty lame, but her mother might buy it. She tried a fake sneeze, but it came out sounding as if she were strangling.

Mrs. Tate held out her hand. "Give me the card, Brittany."

Silently Brittany handed over the card. Her full mouth pressed into a stubborn line. She didn't care! Her mother was so mean not to understand. She braced herself for the lecture and the punishment. She only hoped she wouldn't be grounded that weekend. She couldn't be!

But Mrs. Tate didn't explode. Brittany

waited nervously while her mother stared down at the credit card in her hand. "Why did you do this, Brittany?" she asked slowly. "How can you lie to me like this?"

Oh, no. It was so much worse to see her mother hurt, not angry. Brittany felt awful. She hadn't meant to lie to her mother. She hadn't thought about that part at all. Brittany swallowed. "I'm sorry, Mom," she said. "I was planning to charge the dress, I admit it. But I was going to save money and pay you back by the time you got the bill, I promise."

"That's not the point," her mother said with sudden sharpness. "I told you a new dress was out of the question."

Helplessly, Brittany sank down into the chair beside the table. She felt like bursting into tears. "You don't understand," she said in a choked voice.

Her mother sat down next to her. "What don't I understand?" she asked.

The gentleness in her mother's voice gave Brittany hope. "Don't you remember wanting to look pretty at a special dance?" she pleaded. "I worked so hard to get that junior membership at the country club. It took every penny I was able to make. But now that I get to go to functions there, I don't have any money left for new clothes!"

Her mother sighed. "But, Brittany, that was your decision. You knew you'd have less money to spend on clothes if you paid for the membership. And you have a closet full of beautiful things. Your father and I don't deprive you."

"I know, Mom," Brittany admitted with tears in her eyes. "But everybody's seen all my dresses a million times. I want to look special. It's my first big dance there. I have to go stag because I don't have a boyfriend. I just can't stand having to go in an old dress, too." She wiped at her tears with her hand and sneaked a look at her mother. Mrs. Tate was frowning, but she didn't look too angry.

"I didn't realize this dance was so important to you," she said thoughtfully.

Maybe there *was* hope. "It's *crucial,*" Brittany said, sniffing. She looked at her mother hopefully.

Mrs. Tate shook her head slowly. "I'm sorry, but I can't do it, Brittany. I can't catch you doing a bad thing and then reward you by buying you a dress."

Tears gathered in Brittany's dark eyes. Of course her mother wouldn't back down. She'd never been a pushover. "I know," she said helplessly. "I *am* sorry, Mom."

Mrs. Tate stroked Brittany's hair, concern showing on her face. "Maybe there's something else I could do, though. How would you like to wear a dress of mine?"

Her mother had to be kidding. "Yours?" Brittany asked doubtfully.

Mrs. Tate laughed. "Don't worry, it's not awful. And it just might be perfect for you. I wore it to the Roaring Twenties party your father and I went to. It's an antique." Mrs. Tate stood up. "Come into my bedroom and look at it now, before dinner."

"Okay." Reluctantly, Brittany followed her mother down the hall and into her room. Now, not only would she be wearing an old dress, it would be her *mother's* old dress. And she'd hurt her mother's feelings if she refused. It was awful when parents tried to help.

Mrs. Tate hurried to the closet in her bedroom. Pushing aside a rack of clothes, she disappeared into the back of the closet. When she emerged, her cheeks were flushed, and her dark eyes danced. "What do you think?" she asked, flourishing the dress in front of Brittany. "I think it would fit you."

Brittany hesitated. The dress was gorgeous. It was low-waisted, falling straight to the ankles in a sweep of delicate chiffon. It was a silvery color with intricate crystal beading all through it. Nobody had ever worn a dress like that to any dance Brittany had been to. Brittany circled around her mother, thinking hard. If she wanted to be noticed, this was the dress. But it was a big gamble. It was so totally different. Even Robin Fisher had never worn a dress like this. What would Kim say?

A soft smile curved Brittany's lips. What did it matter what Kim said? Boys would love it.

"Mom, I can't believe it," she said slowly. "But I think you just saved my life."

On Friday afternoon the record and tape sale was a smashing success. Everyone got to try new music or trade in records they were tired of. The prices were very low, but the profits were good. Even if the committee made only half the amount on Monday at the lunchtime sale, they have more than enough money to put on the luau in style.

Ellen went to count the proceeds in Coach Dixon's office. She counted the money twice, then counted it again. There was no way she'd give Juliann Wade grounds for criticism! She bundled the money in a rubber band and wrote out the deposit slip for the bank right there. Then she sealed the slip and the money in an envelope.

As she was reaching for her purse, there was a knock at the door, and Kevin Hoffman stuck his head in. "Hey, Ellen. Thought I'd stop by and congratulate you. I hear the sale was a big success. You ever want to open a discount store, let me know."

Ellen laughed. "I think we'll have enough money for the luau," she said. She hadn't seen Kevin since the student council meeting when he'd defended her. She'd wanted to thank him after it, but he'd rushed out quickly with Cheryl Worth. "I'm glad you stopped by," she added hesitantly. "I didn't get a chance to thank you for what you did at the meeting yesterday."

Kevin shook his head. "Don't thank me. Juliann was out of line. Everybody knows what a pain she is. Don't even think about it."

Don't even think about it! How she wished it were possible. Ellen stood up and hitched her purse on her shoulder. "You're right. Well, I'll see you."

Kevin didn't move from the doorway, and she had to inch past him. She wondered why Kevin was being so nice to her all of a sudden. Did he feel sorry for her?

"Can I walk you to your locker?" he asked suddenly.

"I'm not leaving school yet. I have to go to the student council room," Ellen said. She pointed to the bank envelope. "I have to lock up the money from the sale. Then I have a meeting with Cheryl. Again."

Kevin grimaced sympathetically. "That Worth girl calls more meetings than a Hollywood producer. Hey, can I walk you to the room, then?" He grinned. "I know it's on the second floor, so you'd have to put up with me for longer."

"I guess I'll survive," Ellen said lightly. Her heart was fluttering as they started down the hall together, and she wondered if her crush was really over.

"Here's what I really wanted to say," Kevin said. "I know you probably don't want people to bring it up. But I wanted to say that I'm sorry about your father."

"That's okay, Kevin," Ellen said. "Thanks."

"I know it must be hard on you. How're you doing, anyway?"

Ellen sighed as they began to climb the stairs. "I'm okay, I guess. To tell you the truth, I'm more worried about my little sister. She's not handling it very well."

"I didn't know you had a sister," Kevin said.

She nodded. "She's a freshman here. Her name is Suzanne. She's kind of sensitive, and she doesn't have any close friends. It's been tough on her."

"That's too bad," Kevin said. "I have a little sister, too. You can't help feeling protective, right? Even when they hate you for it."

"Exactly," Ellen agreed.

Kevin cleared his throat. "So, are you going to the country club dance Saturday night?"

Ellen shook her head. "I hadn't planned on it. My father joined the club when we moved to River Heights—mostly for business contacts." Ellen stopped awkwardly, remembering what her father's contacts had gotten him into. "But I don't go there much," she concluded lamely.

"Me, neither. I'd much rather go to the movies. How about you?"

"I love movies," Ellen said.

"Well, how do you feel about the movies and me combined?"

Ellen's steps slowed. Was Kevin asking her for a date?

"I don't even have to sit with you. I could sit in the balcony," Kevin joked. "I'll throw the popcorn down at you."

"I—"

Kevin held up his hand. "I promise I won't throw the soda."

Ellen couldn't believe it. Kevin Hoffman was asking her out! A few months ago she would have been in heaven. Even now, she had to admit she still felt pretty good. But how could she go out and have fun when her family was so miserable?

She shook her head. "That's really nice of you, Kevin. But I can't. Thanks, anyway."

"No sweat," Kevin said offhandedly. "There's always a home video. I'll just sit in my room and make microwave popcorn. I do that on a lot of Saturday nights."

Ellen giggled, but she felt disappointed. Kevin didn't seem too upset that she'd turned him down. They'd reached the room, and Ellen immediately locked the envelope in a drawer. After her meeting with Cheryl and the rest of the Clean Up Your School committee, she'd retrieve the envelope and drop it in the bank night-deposit slot on her way home.

"Well, I guess I'll be seeing you," Kevin said. He shifted from one foot to the other and ran a freckled hand through his red-brown hair, messing it up even more.

"Have a good weekend," Ellen said.

"Right. 'Bye."

Kevin was gone before she could register his goodbye. Ellen sighed as she headed to her meeting. It had been nice of Kevin to ask her to the dance Saturday night. But obviously he was just feeling sorry for her. Or else why did he ask her out only after her father got in trouble?

By the time Saturday night arrived, Brittany's nerves were stretched to the breaking point. She changed her clothes three times, from the twenties antique dress to her black strapless and back to the beaded dress again. At the last minute, Brittany was unsure of the dress's effect. She was going stag to the dance, which already took some nerve. Did she have the nerve to carry off the dress, too?

Brittany tried a black velvet headband around her forehead to complete the twenties look, but finally she just brushed out her long dark hair and left it simple. She stepped into her pumps and she was ready.

She sat on the bed for a full ten minutes, nervously tapping her foot. She had already planned to be just a little late to the dance. That way, she could make an entrance.

She drove to the club in her mother's car, shooting nervous glances at her make-up in the rearview mirror. Brittany knew she looked gorgeous, but the real test would come when she saw the reactions of others.

Her planning paid off—she arrived at the dance at the perfect time. The band had just stopped for a break, and everyone turned to stare at Brittany as she swept in, her head high. She tossed her gleaming hair back once, lifted her chin, and slipped out of the black velvet cape her mother had lent her. With a single swirling motion, she draped it over her arm.

Within moments Kim and Samantha rushed to her side. They both had looks of drop-dead envy on their faces. She'd done it! Brittany crowed inwardly.

"Very dramatic entrance," Kim said. Her frosty blue eyes flicked over Brittany's dress, but she didn't say a word. She self-consciously smoothed the full skirt of her new dress. It was bright fuchsia, with elaborate ruffles and lace along the seams. Brittany thought it was hideous.

"I just can't believe your dress," Samantha gushed to Brittany. "It's *so* gorgeous and sophisticated. Where did you find it?"

"I have my secrets," Brittany said.

"Well, you look fantastic," Samantha said. "Doesn't she, Kim?"

"I'd better go dance with Jeremy," Kim said, as if she hadn't heard Samantha. "He looks positively deserted." She rushed away, the skirt of her new dress rustling.

"Don't mind her," Samantha said, dismissing Kim with a wave. "She's just jealous. She thought she was going to steal the show in that new dress of hers."

"You look lovely tonight, too," Brittany said generously. "That soft mauve is definitely you." Samantha's dress was straight and very tight, and, Brittany thought, a little gauche—a little obvious.

"So what's the plan tonight, Brittany?" Samantha asked shrewdly. One light brown eyebrow arched upward. "I'm dying to know who you're after."

"I'm not *after* anybody in particular," Brittany said, her eyes scanning the crowd. She saw Nikki and Niles and Robin and Calvin. Brittany was glad to see that she'd even outshone Robin, who was wearing the same purple lace dress she'd worn to the last country club dance. Nikki looked pure and innocent in a white-and-gold dress. And was that Lara Bennett with Tim Cooper? Now, *that* was news. He deserved the mealymouthed twit.

"Oh, come on, Brittany," Samantha said. "I know you better than that. Who are you looking for?"

"I'm just shopping, Samantha dear," Brittany said distractedly. But just as she finished speaking, she caught sight of Chip Worthington. He had a petite blond girl hanging on his arm. Oh, no, Brittany thought despairingly. He had a girlfriend! Brittany couldn't see her too well, but she was wearing a boring powder blue dress. Chip looked tall and assured, as if he owned the country club. He scanned the room with a bored air.

Brittany willed him to turn around and look at her, but he returned his attention to the frumpy blonde and the rest of his friends. She sighed. She'd have to get Kim to introduce her, but she'd been hoping to avoid involving her.

Over the next hour Brittany didn't get a chance. She was used to being popular, but this was ridiculous. Time after time, she'd be ready to snag Kim to ask her to introduce her to Chip. But just then a boy would ask Brittany to dance, and she'd lose her opportunity.

Finally she saw her chance. Kim and Jeremy were standing on the sidelines, having a soda. Brittany watched as Chip joined them. Jeremy's face darkened in a scowl, but Chip was grinning as he talked. He was probably tormenting Jeremy, Brittany thought. Maybe he wasn't so bad, after all.

Quickly Brittany excused herself from Marshall Fitzgerald, the head of the marching band, who was boring her to tears about his trip to Florida with his parents. She walked quickly across the room to Kim and Jeremy.

"Hi," she interrupted breathlessly. "I haven't had a chance to talk to you guys all night." She fixed her dark eyes on Chip's. "Oh, I'm sorry, am I interrupting?"

"Not at all," Chip said. His clear green eyes flicked over her, and he gave a lazy grin. "Not at all," he repeated. "Who are *you,* and why haven't I met you yet?"

Brittany smiled back. "How about meeting me right now? I'm Brittany Tate," she said.

"Chip Worthington," Chip answered. "That is some dress, Brittany Tate."

"Well, thank you, Chip Worthington."

Kim stirred beside her. She might not be able to stand Chip, but it was clear she didn't like Brittany stealing his attention, either. "Brittany just became a junior member of the club recently," she said.

"That's probably why you don't know her."

Brittany held on to her smile, but she wanted to kick Kim. Did Kim always have to bring up the fact that Brittany had a *junior* membership?

"I suppose you go to school with Pratt, here," Chip said. He casually ran a hand through his straight, side-parted brown hair.

"That's right. Do you go to Talbot?"

"Of course," Chip replied. "If every Worthington didn't enroll, the school would sink right into the ground and collapse. We practically built the place back in the Stone Age. Now we just throw pots of money at it to keep it running."

Brittany laughed her silvery laugh. What a snob! she thought. Kim was right, for once. "Well, thank heavens you enrolled, then," she said. "We wouldn't want anything to happen to Talbot."

"For sure," Chip agreed lazily. "And what do you do at River Heights High, Brittany?"

"Well, I'm on the school paper, the *Record,*" Brittany said. "I have my own column, called 'Off the Record.'"

"Nice name," Chip said. Why did every remark he make sound as though he was making fun of her? But his light green eyes were definitely expressing approval. Did he like her, or not? Brittany wondered.

"Actually," Chip went on, "I'm the editor in chief of the Talbot paper, the *Clarion.* It's a major drag, but it looks good on my transcripts. Harvard wants the well-rounded student and all that."

This might be harder than she'd thought. If there was one thing Brittany took seriously, it was journalism. Imagine someone only working on the school paper because it looked good on his résumé! Still, if Chip was going to Harvard . . .

Brittany swallowed her protest. "I know what you mean," she agreed. She felt her lips getting stiff from holding her smile. "But don't you find it fascinating?"

Chip shrugged. "Talbot has the most sophisticated equipment, of course. We just got some amazing new software for our computers. It makes us into a small publishing concern, really. It's definitely not a small-time operation, if you know what I mean."

"It sounds fascinating," Brittany cooed.

Kim and Jeremy had been standing there, watching the exchange between Chip and Brittany as if it were a tennis match. They both looked mildly horrified that Brittany was getting along so well with the loathsome Chip.

"Why don't you ask Chip if you should write the Ellen Ming story?" Kim asked brightly. "You guys can discuss newspaper ethics, and Jeremy and I can dance."

"See you, old man," Chip said to Jeremy, his eyes never leaving Brittany. "I'll be glad to talk with Brittany about anything."

Kim and Jeremy left, with Kim shooting Brittany a what-are-you-doing look. Brittany ignored her. Quickly she outlined Ellen's story to Chip, without mentioning names. Should she print it?

"Sure," Chip said, shrugging. "It's news. I don't know why you'd hesitate at all. That's the way the news business is these days. *Everything* is printable."

Brittany didn't think she agreed with that, but she never argued with a boy she was trying to land. She nodded. "I guess you're right, Chip. Thanks for helping me decide."

"Anytime. Let me know if you need help with the article. It might be tough to get the right tone," Chip advised loftily.

Don't tell me how to write, you creep, she thought. "I'd love that," Brittany gushed.

Just then the blond girl in the powder blue dress came up to them. Her face was round but pretty, and her thin lips were drawn down in a pout that she probably thought was cute, but Brittany thought it made her look like a flounder.

"Chip, where have you been? Bob and Tad have been looking everywhere for you. You promised to be back in, like, two seconds," the girl said. Her blue eyes slid over Brittany for an instant. Her eyes narrowed disdainfully at Brittany's dress, then switched back to Chip with a hurt look.

"Sorry, Missy. I got involved talking to a fellow journalist. Brittany Tate, Missy Henderson."

"Nice to meet you," Brittany said sweetly. Missy Henderson, she decided, was not much competition. Her pearls might be real, but she was just a little too plump to get away with her strapless dress. Her nose and her teeth looked too tiny in her moon-shaped face, and she had the kind of fair complexion that could get blotchy in the cold or wind. No, Missy would be a push-over, Brittany decided.

"Yes," Missy said vaguely. "Come on, Chip. I want to dance."

"Duty calls," Chip said offhandedly. "I've enjoyed our talk, Brittany. Good luck with your story."

"Thank you," Brittany said demurely. She didn't mind a bit letting Missy walk off with Chip. She'd get him in the end.

Then she frowned, thinking of their conversation. Chip really was a snob. He seemed really shallow, too. She could take him away from Missy, but did she really want him?

Ellen spent an awful weekend sitting around the house, which was eerily quiet except when Suzanne was banging furiously on the piano. The two sisters spent Saturday night and most of Sunday staring bleary-eyed at the TV. Mr. and Mrs. Ming mostly stayed in their room with the door closed.

Monday dragged by at school. Ellen thought she'd be more used to how people were acting around her, either stiff and unnatural or ignoring her. But it wasn't any easier than it had been on Friday.

She was in the hallway on the way to chemistry class when she passed a group with Kim Bishop at its center.

"Hey, Ellen," Kim called out.

Ellen's steps slowed. She didn't want to stop, but Kim had sounded almost friendly. Was she regretting her acid comments from last week?

"There's a father-daughter dance at the club Saturday night," Kim said in the same friendly tone. "Everybody's going."

A father-daughter dance! That was all she needed. Ellen felt tears gather behind her eyes. She would have been proud to go with her father a week ago. Ellen told her legs to move, to continue down the hall, but she felt mesmerized by the frosty blue gleam of Kim Bishop's stare.

Kim gave an elaborate sigh. "Do you think your father will be out on bail by then?"

Ellen swallowed. "He hasn't been arrested," she said.

Kim gave each of the girls around her a significant look. "Not yet," she said, triumph ringing in her voice. "My father's been nice, so far. But he might act soon. He can't protect your father forever."

Protect him? A cluster of mean replies hovered on Ellen's tongue. She wanted to scream. She wanted to slap Kim. But instead she shook her head and just walked on. She couldn't let her father down by losing her temper.

"I just hope her father looks good in stripes," Kim said loudly.

Ellen heard the girls snicker, and she wanted to run. But she forced herself to keep moving at the same pace. She wouldn't let them know how upset she was.

The same threadbare nerves carried her through the rest of the day, but by the final bell, Ellen was exhausted. She hurried to her locker. At least that day she had no meetings and could walk home with Suzanne. Her sister had looked especially down when they had parted that morning. Had her day been as awful as Ellen's?

But it was a different Suzanne who greeted her as Ellen came up. She didn't look happy, exactly, but she did look a little brighter.

"How was your day?" Ellen asked curiously.

Suzanne grimaced. "Awful." She shut her locker and twirled the lock. "But something happened at lunch."

"What?" Ellen asked as they headed for the stairs.

"This girl Maggie asked me to sit at her table. She's really nice, and so are her friends."

Ellen felt a tiny trickle of relief snake through her. Finally someone in the freshman class was showing some kindness and befriending Suzanne.

"That's great, Suzanne," she said. "I'm glad. Listen, I have to stop by the bank and drop off the money from the record sale at lunch today. It won't take long; I'm using the mail deposit slot."

"Fine," Suzanne said. Usually she was a maniac about her practice time at the piano. But that day a small smile was curving her lips, and her eyes looked brighter.

They headed for the bank in the late-afternoon winter sunshine. Ellen loved the way the snow absorbed noise and made the world seem quiet and protective. "What's this Maggie like?" Ellen asked after they'd walked awhile in comfortable silence.

"She's really funny," Suzanne said. "She has red hair and freckles, and she cracks jokes all the time. But they aren't mean jokes or anything. She gave me half of her chicken salad sandwich. And she really seemed interested in my piano playing."

"She sounds nice," Ellen said. "I'm glad you're making a friend."

"She asked me to sit with her and her friends tomorrow, too. I'm so happy I don't have to eat alone! That was so hard. Now *I'm* at one of those tables where people are laughing and talking. And all because of Maggie Hoffman."

Ellen stopped in her tracks. "Maggie *Hoffman?*" she asked. Her voice came out like a squeak. "Does she have an older brother, by any chance?"

"I don't know," Suzanne said. "Come on, Ellen. I have a lot of homework to do before I can practice."

"Right," Ellen said dazedly, starting to walk again. Could Maggie be Kevin Hoffman's little sister? Another redheaded Hoffman was just too much of a coincidence. And if Maggie *was* Kevin's sister, did he have anything to do with her befriending Suzanne?

Ellen sneaked a look at her sister. What would happen when Kevin stopped feeling sorry for them and moved on to other projects? If Maggie was just following her older brother's orders, would she drop Suzanne when her good deed was done? Poor Suzanne! She'd be terribly hurt. Ellen would have to do something about this, and soon.

 8

At the staff meeting for the *Record* Brittany waited impatiently for the routine business to end. She had a proposal for DeeDee Smith, and she couldn't wait to tell her about it.

All day Sunday while she had worked on her Ellen Ming article, she was turning over *the* crucial question in her mind—how was she going to see Chip again? Brittany knew he'd been dazzled, but obviously not enough to ask her out. All she needed was one more meeting to push him over the edge.

Then inspiration had streaked across her mind like a blazing comet. If only DeeDee would go for it. But first, Brittany thought, stifling a yawn, DeeDee had to wrap up the meeting.

Finally DeeDee seemed to be winding down. "That's about it," she said, looking down at her notes.

"DeeDee?"

Brittany almost groaned out loud. It was Karen Jacobs, probably with some pesky and boring question about production matters.

"What is it, Karen?"

"I've heard a disturbing rumor that I'd like to bring out in the open here," Karen said. "It's going around school that Brittany is writing an article on Ellen Ming and her problem."

Brittany nearly fell off her chair. "So?" she asked huffily.

DeeDee frowned. "What's your angle, Brittany?"

"I haven't finished the article yet," Brittany said defensively. "But I do think it's news that should be reported."

"I think it's terrible," Karen said. She shot a poisonous look at Brittany. "Mr. Ming's troubles have nothing to do with the school, and an article about it would only hurt and embarrass Ellen. It's malicious."

"I don't want to hurt Ellen," Brittany

said, defending herself. "I think it would be strange if we didn't print anything. It's been all over the news—Sheila O'Dell even reported it on the evening news."

"So what?" Karen countered. "That news was about Mr. Ming—not Ellen. It doesn't belong in our school paper."

"Oh, do you want to write another article about the school bake sale, Karen?" Brittany asked her acidly. "That should win us an award for excellence from the Council of High School Newspapers."

"I just don't believe in the kind of journalism you practice, Brittany," Karen shot back angrily. "Before this, it's just been your methods that have been low-down. Now you've moved on to smear tactics in your reporting."

Brittany opened her mouth to shoot a reply back to Karen, but DeeDee raised her hand and gave her a warning look.

"Okay, that's enough," she said crisply. "I think we should table this discussion. Brittany, I want you to show me what you have so far. Maybe I'll take it to Mr. Greene. But I'm warning you, I'm against printing it. I agree with Karen. Okay, that's it, people. Don't forget your deadlines. Have a good one."

Brittany slammed her notebook shut.

Now she was bothered and upset, thanks to Karen's snotty comments.

She took a couple of deep breaths to compose herself, then went up to DeeDee.

"Do you have a minute?" she asked.

DeeDee sighed. "I consider the discussion closed, Brittany, so—"

"It's not about my article," Brittany broke in hastily. "It's about the paper in general. Saturday night I was talking to a student from Talbot about the new software system they have for the *Clarion*. You know how their paper is always getting awards. Maybe we could learn something from their operation."

DeeDee gave a short nod. "So what are you driving at?"

"I know the editor in chief," Brittany said. "He invited me to take a look at what they have. I could come back and report to you on the new software system, and maybe we could talk to Mr. Greene about getting it. If we think we could use it, that is."

DeeDee shook her head slowly. "Brittany, we don't have the kind of budget Talbot does. That's a very rich school. We have only one computer here—and that's for composing. As you know, we all write on typewriters. What good would the software do us?"

"It could save us time and money," Brittany said forcefully. "At least it's worth a look. I was thinking Mr. Greene could get permission for me to leave a little early one day this week. Then I could check it out."

DeeDee thought for a moment. "Okay," she agreed finally. "It's worth a shot. I'll talk to Mr. Greene. You can take Karen with you."

"Karen?" Brittany blurted out. She'd rather die!

DeeDee gave her an exasperated look. "Karen *is* production editor, Brittany. She probably knows a lot more than you do about this stuff. And as long as we're on the subject, I don't like what went on in the meeting today. I don't like bad feelings among the staff. It's time you and Karen got along. This might be a good opportunity for that."

"You're right, DeeDee," Brittany said in what she hoped sounded like a penitent tone. If she had to drag Karen along to Talbot, she would. Actually it might work out. Karen could take all the notes on the software program. And Brittany could concentrate all of her attention on Chip Worthington. Her plan was in motion!

* * *

Tuesday at lunch Kim couldn't stop talking about the father-daughter dance at the country club.

"Here's the greatest thing about it," Kim said flatly. "It's the one time I won't have to go crazy looking for a new dress. *Any* dress is the perfect dress in my father's eyes."

Brittany didn't answer. She poked doubtfully at the burrito on her plate. The cafeteria's idea of Mexican Fiesta Day left something to be desired. She should have gone for the tuna surprise. And she wished Kim would stop bringing up the father-daughter dance! How nerdy could you get. There was no way Brittany was going to ask her father to go to a country club event with her. He was sweet, but totally inept in social situations. He'd probably spill a drink down her dress or embarrass her in some horrible way.

"My father is really looking forward to it," Kim went on, cutting her shrimp salad sandwich into quarters.

"Mine says he is," Samantha said, reaching for the salt. "But I don't know, he hates to dance. I'm only going because you twisted my arm, Kim."

"How about your dad, Brittany?" Kim asked, picking up a sliver of her sandwich. "Is he looking forward to it?"

"I told you a million times, Kim. I'm not going. I think it's a totally gross idea. I'd rather stay home and study French than dance with my father." Brittany took a tentative bite of burrito. It wasn't too bad.

"Are you sure that's the real reason you don't want to go, Brittany?" Kim asked with a malicious spark in her ice blue eyes.

Brittany paused, wondering how a beef burrito would look on top of Kim's perfectly combed blond hair. Kim was trying to suggest that Brittany was ashamed of her father. And she wasn't—not really. She just cringed when she thought of him mingling with Mr. Masters.

"Actually, Kim," she said coolly, "I think it's pretty lousy how you're harping on this dance. Last year you said it was one big yawn, and this year you're talking it up like it was a prom or something. I think you're just trying to get back at Ellen Ming. You just want to rub it in her face that her father is under suspicion."

"Correction," Kim said flatly. "He's guilty. And if I'm proud of my father, why shouldn't I show it? It has nothing to do with Ellen and her father."

"Shhh, Kim," Samantha hissed. "Lower your voice. Ellen is coming."

But instead of lowering her voice, Kim talked louder. "I don't care," she said.

"Mr. Ming will be in jail soon, anyway. And aren't you being a little hypocritical, Brittany? You're putting the whole story in the *Record,* aren't you?"

Behind Kim, Brittany saw Ellen slow down. Her hands gripped the cafeteria tray, her knuckles growing white. Then she moved on quickly.

"That's enough, Kim," Brittany snapped. "I don't know if the story is going in the *Record* or not. What's wrong with you, anyway? Why do you have to rub Ellen's nose in this every chance you get?"

"You're just upset because your darling Chip Worthington hasn't called you," Kim said spitefully. "I saw the way you threw yourself at him at the dance."

"As a matter of fact, I talked to Chip last night," Brittany said with forced casualness. She *had* talked to Chip. But she'd been the one to call him. She'd had to clear things with Chip about her visit to Talbot before Mr. Greene asked Mr. Meacham about it. So she'd told Chip that her editor had suggested the field trip to Talbot.

Chip had been friendly, but he let it slip that Missy was over on a study date. That hadn't been very good news, but at least he'd sounded glad that he would see her again.

"So," Kim said. "He's your latest conquest, is he? Good luck, Brittany. It's a good thing you don't have much of a gag reflex. He's awfully hard to swallow, isn't he?"

Samantha pushed back her curly brown bangs and pressed her fingers against her temples. "Will you two stop it, please? I'm getting a headache. All you do these days is argue. It's bad enough I have to sit with Kyle's friends twice a week, listening to them talk about positive ions and iambic pentameter. When I finally get to sit here and have a normal conversation without Kyle for once, you two argue the whole time!" She gazed at them, her cinnamon brown eyes wide. "Cut it out!"

"All right," Brittany muttered. She stabbed her burrito with her fork. Wait until she saw Chip Worthington at Talbot the next day. Mr. Meacham had approved the plan, and she and Karen would get to leave school a half hour early.

Soon Chip would be hers. That would really annoy Kim. So what if Brittany wasn't sure if she liked him or not? Kim couldn't stand him, and that would drive her absolutely nuts!

Ellen banged her tray down on Karen and Ben's table harder than she'd meant to do.

"What's the matter, Ellen?" Karen asked, sounding concerned.

"Is it true?" Ellen whispered, sinking into a chair. "Is Brittany really going to write an article about my father for the *Record?*"

Karen looked guilty. "I didn't tell you about it because I knew you'd be upset. It's not for sure yet. DeeDee is still deciding, and she said she was against it. Don't worry, DeeDee won't let her print anything malicious."

"I guess it shouldn't matter," Ellen said tiredly. "But it does. Seeing it in black and white like that. And I keep hoping that some of the kids and teachers don't know yet."

"I'm sorry, Ellen," Karen said.

"DeeDee probably won't let it get by," Ben said.

"What if everyone reads it, and they think like Juliann Wade?" Ellen asked, her face paling at the thought. "What if they don't let me be class treasurer anymore?" She stood up suddenly. "I couldn't stand that!"

"Ellen, calm down," Karen said urgently. "Nothing like that will happen."

"You don't know that!" Ellen said. She grabbed her leather knapsack. "Listen, I can't eat. I'm going to the library to study." Before Karen or Ben could stop her, Ellen had turned away.

She rushed out of the cafeteria, her head down. But as she reached the door, she heard someone call her name.

"Ellen! Wait up!"

Ellen had to turn. It was Kevin Hoffman. He grinned amiably at her as he came toward her.

"Hi," he said. "I just wanted to see how you were doing."

Suddenly Ellen felt angry. She couldn't stand one more person feeling sorry for her. And she'd almost forgotten her concern about Suzanne. "Actually, I'm not great right now," she said frostily. "And I want to talk to you about something."

"Sure," Kevin said. His reddish eyebrows drew together in a puzzled frown. "What's up?"

"My sister, Suzanne, told me yesterday that she has a new friend. Her name is Maggie. Maggie Hoffman."

Kevin grinned happily. "Well, you told me you were worried about your sister. And Maggie's a good kid. I just asked her to be nice to Suzanne. You don't have to thank me."

"I'm not thanking you," Ellen said crisply. "I'm telling you it's none of your business."

Kevin's grin slowly faded. "What?"

"What's going to happen when my father is cleared, or goes to jail, or whatever is going to happen to him? What's going to happen when it's old news? Suzanne thinks she's found a real friend. She'll be destroyed when Maggie drops her."

"That's not going to happen," Kevin protested. "Maggie is—"

"A good kid. I heard. But she didn't befriend Suzanne before my father was in trouble. And you didn't have the time of day for me before, either. So," Ellen said in a choked voice, "I want to thank you and your sister for all your kind attention. And I also want you to leave us alone!"

She swung her head around to avoid Kevin's shocked face. Then, clutching her books, Ellen ran, tears streaming down her face. The words had spilled out of her without her controlling them at all. She didn't know if she even meant them. What was happening to her?

9

Finally Wednesday afternoon arrived and Brittany left P.E. early. She spent a while freshening up her makeup before running out to meet Karen in the parking lot. She grinned at her reflection as she brushed out her long dark hair. She did look fabulous —even after a gym class.

She'd spent a lot of time picking out her outfit, and she knew it was perfect. She was wearing a black wool miniskirt with a red turtleneck and a silver chain belt. Her black-and-white tweed jacket was the best one she owned. Tiny pearl earrings were in her ears. They weren't real, but who could tell? Missy wouldn't be there to peer at them. She went to Fox Hill, the exclusive sister school to Talbot. Brittany's dark eyes danced. Finally she'd have Chip all to herself.

Well, almost, she amended as she walked outside and saw Karen waiting for her. But Karen was so wrapped up in Ben Newhouse, she wouldn't even notice that Chip was a boy.

Karen didn't even say hello. She was still angry at Brittany about the Ellen Ming article, even though DeeDee had decided to kill it. Secretly Brittany had been relieved. She had felt uneasy about printing the news in the *Record* from the very beginning and probably wouldn't have written the article at all if she hadn't wanted to show it to Chip.

"Let's go," Karen said brusquely. "We have to get the number three bus."

"I know," Brittany snapped. Those were the last words they exchanged before they reached Talbot.

Brittany and Karen went to the office to sign in and get passes, and the secretary paged Chip. He arrived in a few moments, dressed in the Talbot blue blazer, striped tie, and gray flannel slacks. Brittany was impressed. Nobody at River Heights High ever looked that good for school. She smiled her hello at Chip and introduced him to Karen.

"Welcome, ladies," Chip said as he led them down the hall. "This will be quite a treat for the monastery, here."

A bell rang, signaling the end of the last period. Classroom doors opened and boys spilled out. "I think you're in for a good visit," Chip went on, ignoring the stares of the passing boys, as though he always walked the halls of Talbot with a girl on either side of him. "We have a very sophisticated setup at the *Clarion.* It's important for the prestige of the school, you know. Most of us are going on to Ivy League colleges, so we have to have the best."

"Of course," Brittany murmured. She could barely concentrate on Chip. She'd gone into boy overload, that was for sure. All around her were boys in gray flannel pants and blue wool blazers. Tall boys, short boys, cute boys, muscular boys. Brown hair and black hair and blond hair. And they were all looking at her!

Brittany tossed back her gleaming hair and smiled at each of them. Maybe the software system would be so fascinating that she'd have to pay a return visit. Why hadn't she realized what fun a boys' school would be? She'd never had so many admiring glances in such a short period of time before. She was practically dizzy!

Besides, she told herself as she gave a

flirtatious look to a tall, handsome boy, it would help with Chip if all his friends told him what a knockout she was.

She was almost disappointed when they reached the *Clarion* office. It was empty except for a nerdy-looking boy at one of the computers.

"Terence is our resident expert on the software," Chip said in a bored tone. "So he can show you the nuts and bolts. Right, old man?" He managed to imply that the nuts and bolts were made for dull fellows like Terence.

"Be glad to," Terence said. He gave Chip a disgusted look, but he positively beamed at Brittany and Karen. His braces gleamed and his brown eyes shone eagerly.

Brittany returned a strained smile. "I think that's really Karen's department," she said quickly. "She's the production editor. Why don't you show me some of your clippings, Chip, while Karen talks to Terence?"

Chip nodded. "Sounds like an excellent idea, Brittany. Come with me."

For the next half hour Brittany listened to an endless recital of all the articles Chip had worked on since his freshman year. Chip seemed to find himself the most thrilling topic around. Brittany nodded and smiled until her cheeks ached. She almost jumped up and gave a cheer when Karen came over and interrupted them.

"I've got to go, Brittany. I'm supposed to meet Ben at the mall."

There was no way she was walking out with Karen. "Chip was just showing me an article on the pressures of high school athletics," Brittany said quickly. "I thought it might be a good follow-up to the cheating ring story at River Heights High. Why don't you go on ahead?"

Karen shrugged. "Okay. I'll see you." As Chip took a stray folder back to the filling cabinet, she leaned over to Brittany. "You don't mind staying here with that jerk?" she whispered.

Brittany shot her an angry look, but Karen wasn't trying to rile her. She didn't know Brittany was interested in Chip. "No," she muttered. "You can go, Karen."

Karen left, and Brittany had to endure fifteen more minutes of going over Chip's articles. But finally he wound down. "Well, that's it," Chip said, standing up. "I hope you picked up some good pointers."

"Absolutely," Brittany said. "You're a terrific writer, Chip."

"I try," he said. "Let me walk you out, Brittany." He grabbed his coat and books.

Brittany was quiet as she walked through the halls with Chip. She had thought the afternoon would go a bit differently. Chip hadn't asked her one question about herself. He hadn't suggested they get together. She still didn't know if he would ever call her. And she wanted to be sure! She didn't want to sit around for the rest of the week, staring at the phone and waiting for it to ring.

He liked her, Brittany knew. He thought she was pretty. So why didn't he ask her out?

When they reached the stone steps at the front of the school, Brittany pulled out all the stops. She gave him a melting look from under her eyelashes. "That was quite an experience," she said. "I had a good time."

"Me, too," Chip agreed. "Maybe your editor will suggest a follow-up visit."

Or maybe you should ask me for a date, you jerk. "You could come and see our setup at River Heights High," Brittany suggested.

Chip gave a short laugh. "I don't think so, Brittany. But," he said, moving a little closer and staring down into her eyes, "I wouldn't mind seeing you again."

Brittany smiled up at him. "Oh?" she asked breathlessly.

"Chip!" The voice was high-pitched and

a little shrill. It was also depressingly familiar. "I'm over here."

Brittany looked across the steps to the curb. Missy was sitting in a blue Mercedes that matched her eyes. She was wearing a kelly green coat that made her cheeks look too ruddy.

"It's Missy," Chip said. "Come on over and say hello."

"Sure," Brittany trilled. "I'd love to." Keeping a smile on her face, she trailed behind Chip. Was Missy a steady girlfriend? she wondered irritably. She sure seemed to be Velcroed to Chip.

"You remember Brittany, don't you?" Chip asked her.

Missy tilted her head and smiled. "Of course I do," she said. "From the club. Isn't it funny how you never see someone, and then all of a sudden they're just *everywhere?*"

"I know just what you mean," Brittany answered, smiling back with the same insincere sweetness.

"Well, you know I'd love to chat, but, Chip, we have to get to the club." She turned to Brittany. "We're playing doubles on the indoor court with my brother, Reed, and his fiancée, Merry. My family and Chip's family are so incredibly close. Chip and I grew up together. We've been going steady since we were practically *infants.*"

"How nice for you," Brittany said. "You didn't have to worry about a date for the kindergarten prom."

Chip guffawed and looked at her appreciatively. "Very funny," he said.

Missy closed her eyes for a split second, as if she were in pain. "Right," she said. "Well, hope to see you at the club again, Brittany. Maybe at the father-daughter dance this weekend? Does my father know yours?" Missy frowned, as if she were thinking hard. "I don't think so. Oh, well. We really *have* to go, Chip. You know how Reed and Merry are when we're late."

"Right," Chip said. He went around to the passenger side. He grinned at her. "Goodbye, Brittany. I'll see you real soon."

"Goodbye, Chip. 'Bye, Missy." Brittany smiled and waved as they drove off. She felt like stamping her feet and screaming. He would have asked her out if that girl hadn't shown up! Well, she wasn't worried, despite Missy's veiled reference to the zero social standing of Brittany's family. She wouldn't give Missy a chance to be condescending—she wasn't going to the dance at the club. And she could tell by the last look she'd received from those cool green eyes that she'd landed Chip. Missy would be history very soon!

On Wednesday night Ellen placed the last dinner dish in the rack. She'd refused any help with the dishes after dinner. All she wanted was to be alone to bury her hands in hot soapy water and scrub away at food particles on the saucepans. All she wanted to think about was getting the glasses sparkling clean. She didn't want to think about the shocked look on Kevin Hoffman's face when she'd told him to leave her alone.

Sighing, she wiped her hands on a dish towel. She hadn't meant to be mean to Kevin. He was just trying to be nice, to do her a good turn, but she couldn't stand people feeling sorry for her. Especially not Kevin!

Ellen climbed the stairs to her room with a can of soda. Well, she had enough work to keep her mind off Kevin. A nice fat statement had arrived from the bank that day, and she had to balance the junior class's books. That should take her most of the evening.

She felt better when she reached her room. Her mother had helped her decorate it, and Ellen loved how serene it was. The walls were white, and the nubby bedspread was white with a purple border. An old wicker trunk sat at the end of the bed. Ellen didn't have plants or posters like other girls. She liked things simple and neat. She only had one framed art print on the wall over her bed. There was an antique desk in one corner with a modern black lamp on it. Black high-tech bookshelves lined one wall, with all her books, a small TV, and her tape player on the shelves. Just entering the room made Ellen feel calm.

She got out her calculator and the junior class ledger book from her backpack. First, she would balance the bank statement, then check the amount against what she had entered in the ledger. Ellen bent over her work, losing track of time. She loved the precision of numbers. She loved how they always worked out. Even when they didn't seem to, numbers always made sense.

Ellen finished balancing the statement, then turned to her ledger. Her finger ran down the list of deposits and checks written. Most of the checks were for Winter Carnival expenses, but this week there had been only deposits from the record and tape sale. She turned the page and read the last number she had recorded as her balance.

Ellen frowned. She turned back to the balance the bank said was in the account. The two numbers weren't the same! The bank had less money in the account than Ellen thought was there. A *lot* less.

A chill ran through her. She told herself not to panic. She must have added up the numbers wrong. She'd been upset lately, hadn't she? With shaking fingers, she entered the numbers from the ledger into the calculator. She got the same total, so she did it again.

Ellen threw down her pencil and stared at her figures. It couldn't be. But numbers didn't lie. *Numbers always made sense.* There was money missing from the junior class account!

10

The next day Brittany caught up with DeeDee while she was practicing fencing in the gym. DeeDee raised her meshed mask and nodded while Brittany gave her a quick rundown on the trip to Talbot.

"So," Brittany concluded, "Karen has most of the information on the software system."

DeeDee looked at her curiously. "I thought you were interested in the software, Brittany."

"Well, sure. But since Karen is production editor, I didn't want to step on her toes," Brittany said virtuously. "Anyway, I was glad to look into it for the *Record.*"

DeeDee gave a half smile while she

practiced lunging. "Right, Brittany. You were glad to get off a half hour early from school and go to an all-boys school and talk to rich guys. It must have been torture for you."

Brittany grinned. DeeDee had her number, all right. It was hard to bluff her sharp editor in chief, so she might as well be good-natured about it. Besides, DeeDee *was* holding a foil. "I managed to survive the ordeal," Brittany said archly.

DeeDee laughed and started to pull her mask down again. Then she stopped and raised it again. "Oh, I almost forgot. Two things. I have to admit I was disappointed in you when you submitted that article on Ellen Ming. The *Record* would never print allegations about a student's father. I don't want to see anything like that again from you, Brittany."

She *knew* that article would get her in trouble! It was all Kim's fault. Brittany fervently hoped it wouldn't spoil her chances for next year. Her only recourse was a bit of flattery. "I know, DeeDee," she said sincerely. "That's why I rely on your judgment. But I'm learning."

DeeDee looked at her skeptically. "Okay, Brittany. Just consider it a warning, all right? Here's the second thing.

About next week's paper. I was thinking a story on tomorrow night's father-daughter dance at the country club might be fun."

"You've got to be kidding," Brittany said.

"No, really," DeeDee said. Her velvety brown eyes had that no-nonsense look. "For some reason, a lot of kids are going this year. I'm going to have Nikki take her camera and get some shots. I want you to interview girls, ask them about their fathers, if they do things together, stuff like that. Keep it light and fun."

"But I'm not going," Brittany protested.

DeeDee frowned. "I thought you were a member of the club."

"Well, yes. But—"

DeeDee tapped her lightly on the arm with her foil. "Then you're going, kiddo."

DeeDee put her mask down and went back to practicing her parries and lunges. Brittany frowned and headed out of the gym. Her assignment was not good news. What was she going to do? She'd have to come up with an excuse for DeeDee. Her father could have an unexpected business trip, or a funeral, or something.

She'd get out of it somehow, Brittany vowed as she headed to the cafeteria. Missy Henderson would be there. Missy would be sure to tell Chip what a total zero

Brittany's father was. And now that Brittany was close to landing him, she couldn't afford any slipups. Missy was out for blood. There was no way Brittany could go to that dance!

Ellen didn't go to the cafeteria for lunch. Instead, she brought a few crackers and an apple to the locker room and ate there quickly, then went to the library for the rest of the period. She was terrified that someone—Juliann, or Ms. Rose, or even Ben—would ask her how the luau fund was coming along. Ellen was no good at lying.

She stared with unseeing eyes at her social studies textbook. What was she going to do? She hadn't made a mistake with the books. Someone was tampering with the junior-class funds. It wasn't her, but everyone would think it was! Ellen shuddered, thinking of Kim Bishop. Kim was so spiteful. What would she do if she ever found out about this?

Nobody could find out, Ellen vowed. But she couldn't tackle the problem alone. Usually she went to her parents when she was in trouble, but she couldn't this time. They had enough to worry about. Ellen frowned. But who could she trust? Karen and Ben, certainly. But Ben was junior-class president and on the student council. It would put him in an awkward position. He might feel he had to go to Ms. Rose and tell her, or at least urge Ellen to go. And she couldn't tell Ms. Rose!

Suddenly Ellen thought of Nikki Masters. Nikki had been in trouble once, when her boyfriend was murdered and she was accused of the crime. She knew what real trouble was. And Ellen knew instinctively that Nikki could keep a secret. She'd talk to her right after school.

Ellen was relieved when Nikki agreed to her mysterious request after only a slight hesitation. Ellen asked her not to ask any questions until they were alone. They both climbed into Nikki's car, and Nikki followed Ellen's directions to a coffee shop near the business district. Ellen knew that Nikki was curious, but she didn't ask any questions.

Nikki parked the car and followed Ellen into the coffee shop. After they ordered sodas, Nikki looked at her expectantly.

"What's on your mind, Ellen?"

Nikki's blond hair was shining in the sun coming through the window. She leaned forward, her hands cupping her glass. Her blue eyes were kind and patient. Ellen suddenly felt afraid. Nikki Masters had been in trouble once—that was true. But she was well past it now. She was beautiful and popular, and nice, too. Would she be able to sympathize with Ellen's problem?

"Ellen, if it makes it any easier for you, I know what it's like to need help," Nikki said softly. "I know it's hard to ask. But believe me, it's better. I want to do what I can."

Ellen's fears dissolved under the balm of Nikki's soft words. She gripped her glass and poured out her story, barely pausing for breath.

"I've gone over the books more times than you can imagine," Ellen concluded. "I discovered right away that two deposits I recorded in the ledger didn't match with the bank's record of deposits. I even called them to make sure they hadn't made a mistake."

"How do you make deposits?" Nikki asked. "At the bank?"

"No, it closes at three, so I use the night-deposit slot," Ellen told her. "The two deposits were from last Friday and this Monday. I had to make two so close because of the record and tape sale. Each day I totaled the receipts, filled out a deposit slip, and sealed the envelope. Then I locked it in a drawer in the student council office. After school, I took it to the bank."

Nikki nodded thoughtfully. "So somebody got to the money while it was in the drawer. They took out the bills and resealed the envelope."

"That's what I figure," Ellen said. "But, Nikki, who's going to believe that it wasn't me? After what's happened with my father, I mean."

"I believe it wasn't you," Nikki assured her. "Others will, too. Not everybody is like Kim Bishop, Ellen."

"But I'm class treasurer, Nikki. If my name isn't cleared, I'll lose the office."

Nikki sighed. "Nobody can find out about this, I agree. When are you supposed to come up with the money for the luau?"

"Next week," Ellen said. Panic rippled through her voice.

"I have an idea," Nikki said slowly. "Would you mind if one more person knew the story? Not someone from school," she added hastily.

"Who?" Ellen asked, puzzled.

"Nancy Drew. She's a good friend of mine."

"Wow," Ellen breathed. "Do you think it would be okay?"

"We won't know until I call her," Nikki

said briskly. She reached into the pocket of her jeans for some change. "Can I?"

"Right now?" Ellen gulped. "I guess so. How can I turn down a world-famous detective?"

Nikki grinned and slid out of the booth. Ellen saw her dial a number at the pay phone in back. She sipped her soda while Nikki talked, her back to the coffee shop. In a minute Nikki headed toward her with a smile.

"It's all fixed," she said. "We can see her tonight."

"What did you say?" Ellen asked nervously.

"I said a friend of mine was in trouble, and could we talk to her about it." Nikki grinned. "She's used to that. She said sure and asked us to come over tonight. She lives right next door to me. Why don't you come to my house after dinner, and then we'll go over together?"

"Thanks, Nikki," Ellen said fervently. "You're the best."

"Don't thank me yet," Nikki said. "I haven't done anything."

"You listened," Ellen said simply. "And you're on my side. These days, that's quite a lot."

* * *

That night the Tate family was having stir-fried chicken with vegetables. Brittany's mother had cooked everything just a little bit too long, and the vegetables had merged into one limp, unidentifiable mass. As she poked at what might be broccoli, Brittany privately decided that before she had to eat another stir-fried meal, she was going to hide her mother's wok. She'd liked her mother's Italian craze much better.

Tamara poked at her plate. "What's this?"

"Bok choy, dear," her mother replied.

"Yum," Brittany's father said, too heartily. "Delicious."

"Oh, Brittany, I keep meaning to ask you," her mother said. "I hear they're having a father-daughter dance at the country club."

Her father looked up. "A father-daughter dance, huh?"

Brittany wanted to dive right into her plate. What could she say? "Yes, I heard," she said. "But I knew it was the kind of thing that would bore Dad to tears. I know how he feels about the club."

"Bored having a special evening with my daughter?" her father said. His brown eyes beamed at her behind his glasses. "I'd be honored."

"I think it would be great for the two of you to have a night out together," Mrs. Tate said.

"You'd really want to go, Dad? I mean, don't say yes because of me." Brittany couldn't believe it. This had to be the worst. She couldn't hurt her father's feelings. He was the only person in the world who could get her to go to that dance.

"I wouldn't miss it," her father said, beaming.

"Great!" Her mother looked fondly at both of them in turn.

"Great," Brittany echoed weakly. Her heart sank into her shoes. She was trapped. "I can't wait!"

11 

The bitter cold air hit Ellen's face as she slipped out of the house and shut the front door behind her. She was glad to leave her house tonight—her parents hadn't said one word during dinner. In fact, they had looked so worried that Ellen wondered if anything worse had happened. Then, after dinner, Suzanne had told her more stories about her new friend, Maggie Hoffman. Ellen had been torn between worry for Suzanne and agonizing thoughts about Kevin. Finally, she had grabbed her coat and run out of the house.

Nikki was waiting outside when Ellen drove up in her mother's Saab, and the two girls walked across the dark lawn to the brightly lit Drew house. Nancy Drew opened the door. She was wearing jeans and a cotton turtleneck and didn't look much like a famous detective. She looked like the pretty, athletic girls Ellen saw at the country club.

But when Nancy reached out to shake her hand as Nikki introduced them, Ellen felt the penetrating gaze of Nancy's blue eyes. She could tell by the firm handshake, quiet voice, and keen intelligence in her eyes that Nancy Drew *was* different.

"Let's go up to my room," Nancy suggested. "I have some soda and popcorn up there."

But nobody ate the popcorn or touched the sodas while Ellen poured out her story. She started with her father's troubles, then moved on to her own. Nancy listened, occasionally asking a question or gently bringing Ellen back to the facts if she got off the track.

When she was done, Ellen felt tired, as if she had just run a mile. Nancy popped open a can of soda and handed it to her. "Here," she said, her blue eyes twinkling. "I think you deserve this."

Ellen took it gratefully. "Thanks."

Nancy handed a can to Nikki, then took one for herself. But she didn't open it. She turned it around and around in her slender hands while she talked.

"First of all," she began, "you and your father have the same problem. Someone on the inside is stealing money, and both of you are in a position that naturally draws suspicion. The trick is to figure out who else had access to the money. Actually, for your father that's easier to do. There can be only a handful of people at your father's firm who could have juggled funds and maybe a couple of people on Mr. Bishop's end—including Mr. Bishop."

"You mean Mr. Bishop could have lied—that he could have taken his own money?" Ellen asked doubtfully.

Nancy shrugged. "It happens. He could be hiding money from his partners or the government, you never know. But I don't think that's the case here. Everything points to the trouble being at your father's firm. What I think we should do is get my father involved."

Carson Drew was a prominent attorney, even more famous than Mr. Bishop's attorney. "You mean he'd take our case?" Ellen asked breathlessly.

"I can't speak for him," Nancy said. "But I *will* talk to him. It sounds like something he'd like to get involved in. Now, let's talk about you, Ellen." Nancy frowned. "Unfortunately, I'm going out of town tomorrow, so I can't investigate this myself. But I think you and Nikki should be able to catch the culprit."

"But how?" Ellen asked. "I wouldn't know where to begin."

There was so much distress in Ellen's voice that Nancy reached over and patted her knee. "Don't worry, Ellen. I really do think you guys can solve this on your own. There's no great secret to being a good detective. For this particular case, you need only one strategy. And it's the simplest one of all."

"What's that?" Nikki asked.

Nancy popped open her soda and grinned. "Keep your eyes open," she advised. Then she leaned forward and began to tell the girls her plan.

Brittany hated to work out at any time of day or night. But this time she made an exception. After dinner she packed her workout gear and left for the country club. By the next night, Missy could spoil all her plans. Brittany had to get Chip to ask her out before then. She had to draw him into her web before he found out how socially backward her family was.

There was a good chance Chip would be at the club, she knew. Jeremy had said that Chip was there almost every night. Brittany hated to look as if she was chasing him, but she had no choice. She had to catch him without Missy around.

Chip wasn't in the workout room, but he might be in the men's gym or the steam room. Brittany lifted a few weights and then stopped. She didn't want to get all sweaty. She was wearing a new blue leotard, and she wanted to look fresh. She hung a pink towel around her neck and ambled toward the juice bar to plan her strategy. It was only eight o'clock. She had two hours before her parents would call out the dogs.

But luck was with her. She was sipping her pineapple-banana juice when Chip walked in. He was alone—finally.

He saw her immediately, and his eyes brightened, she was sure of it. But his stride was unhurried as he came over to her table.

"Well, if it isn't Brittany Tate," he said. "What are you doing here alone?"

"I just had my workout," Brittany said. "And you?"

He grinned. "My kind of workout. A quick poker game with some friends. I quit early. Wasn't feeling very lucky." He slid into the seat next to hers. "But I think I just changed my mind."

Brittany toyed with her straw. "Where's Missy?" she asked.

Chip grinned. "Who?" His green eyes moved over her lazily.

She smiled. "Your girlfriend," she said pointedly. "You know, the one who's practically part of the family?"

"Oh, right. Missy's home polishing her nails or something. We go out sometimes, but that girl loves to tie strings. I'm a little tired of it."

"You didn't look very tired of it today," Brittany pointed out.

"Believe me, Brittany, I was more interested in tennis than Missy today."

"It's just that I was hoping we'd have a chance to talk more," Brittany said, pouting a little. She'd show that rank amateur Missy Henderson what a real pout was. Brittany looked up at Chip from under her lashes.

Chip's hand slid over hers. "Actually, I was thinking the same thing. Where have you been all my life, Brittany?" he asked. His eyes were half-closed as he gazed down at her. "Looking for me, I hope," he added with a laugh. Brittany's smile tightened slightly. What a conceited jerk! But her eyes continued to gaze adoringly at him. She wished he'd ask her for a date so she could go home and get some sleep. Her pursuit of him was wasting too much energy.

"So, Brittany, are we going to go out together?" Chip asked.

At last! "Well, I'm not sure. You tell me, Chip," she returned flirtatiously.

"How about Saturday night?" he asked. "Dinner here at the club, and then Commotion? I never got to dance with you the other night, you know. I still haven't gotten over it."

Brittany looked at him shrewdly. "I bet you already have a date Saturday night," she said.

"I bet you do, too," Chip said. "Why don't we break those dates?"

Brittany didn't have a date Saturday night. She'd kept it open for Chip. But he didn't have to know that. "Consider it broken," she said softly. She took a sip of her juice and smiled at Chip.

Wait until Missy found out! No matter what happened Friday night, Brittany had Chip lined up for Saturday. And no matter how spiteful Missy was, Brittany wouldn't have to worry. She could tell by the gleam in Chip's eyes that she'd landed him. Kim would flip. Chip was the biggest fish in town!

By the time Ellen drove home, the hope she'd felt at Nancy Drew's was wearing off. Nancy had been so helpful. She'd generously given Ellen and Nikki all kinds of tips on catching the culprit. But as Ellen pulled into the driveway, she felt depressed again.

Nothing had changed. She was no better off than she had been earlier really. She still had to come up with the money for the luau, and her father could still go to jail.

She looked up at her family's house. All the lights were on. Then she noticed the black late-model car in front of the house. Maybe it was an unmarked police car!

Ellen's heart began to pound. Her hands shook as she turned off the ignition and threw the keys into her purse. She pushed open the car door and hesitated in the driveway. Something was wrong, she just knew it! Throwing her purse over her shoulder, Ellen ran for her front door.

She burst into the house wildly. Her father, her mother, Suzanne, and Mr. Sachs, their lawyer, were sitting in the living room. Ellen noticed that her mother was crying.

"Ellen?" Her mother rose quickly to her feet. "Honey, what is it?"

"You tell me," Ellen said, breathing heavily from her run and her anxiety. "What happened? What's wrong?"

Mrs. Ming smiled. Tears glistened on her black lashes. "Nothing's wrong, honey. Everything's very right. Your father has been cleared of all charges! Mr. Sachs came over to tell us personally."

For a moment Ellen didn't feel anything. Then a rush of relief so intense it made her dizzy washed over her. "He's cleared?" she whispered, her purse dropping to the floor. "I thought he was going to jail," she said dazedly. Her gaze moved from one face to another and came to rest on her father's. He smiled.

"Oh, Daddy." Ellen rushed across the room and threw her arms around him. "I'm so, so happy. How did it happen?"

"It was your father who did it," Mr. Sachs said in a satisfied way. "He went over and over the case. He followed the money trail. He finally had to conclude it was Mr. Pope."

Ellen sat up straight. "Your partner?" she asked, shocked. "But, Daddy, how could he? You two are friends."

"Honey, it's a sad thing, but money can affect some people in destructive ways," Mr. Ming said. "Once they get a taste of it, they don't care what stands in their way. Even friendship."

"So once we zeroed in on our man," Mr. Sachs went on, "we started to gather the evidence. It's difficult to hide money if someone looks hard enough for it. I went over to Mr. Pope's tonight with the evidence we'd gathered, and he confessed. He's already called Mr. Bishop. The charges against your father have all been dropped."

"I thought I'd open some champagne," Mrs. Ming said happily. "Can you stay, Mr. Sachs?"

"Wouldn't miss it."

"Can I have some, Mom?" Suzanne asked. "I've never tasted champagne."

"A sip," her mother said. "This is a happy night."

Ellen sat close to her father, feeling safe for the first time in days. "I can't believe it," she said. "I just went to talk to Nancy Drew. She's going to mention your case to her father." She turned to Mr. Sachs with a grin. "No offense, Mr. Sachs. I know you're a great lawyer. I just thought the more people on my father's side, the better."

"No offense taken," Mr. Sachs said. He pushed up his glasses and smiled. "I would have been happy to work with Carson Drew. But I'm even happier that the case never came to trial."

Her father squeezed her hand. "Thanks, sweetheart. I appreciate the help."

"The nightmare is over," Mrs. Ming said. "Now things can get back to normal."

Back to normal. Ellen's heart started to beat nervously again. There was no "back to normal" for her. Her life was still upside down. Her father had been cleared, but another big problem still remained. How would she catch the thief at school?

She remembered her father's words: "They don't care what stands in their way. Even friendship." Suddenly Ellen realized that she must know the culprit. She shivered at the thought. Who would turn out to be the thief at River Heights High?

12

The next day, Friday, Ellen woke up realizing that it wouldn't be torture to go to school. She still had her own problem, of course. But for the first time in a while she could walk the halls without being afraid of people staring at her. And if she saw Kim Bishop she wouldn't have to turn a corner to avoid her. She could walk right by Kim and look her straight in the eye.

Suzanne was in a good mood, too. With all the celebrating the night before, the whole family had overslept, so Mrs. Ming had to drive Suzanne and Ellen to school again.

While Suzanne talked to their mother about her new friend, Maggie, Ellen began to feel nervous again. Would Maggie welcome Suzanne just as warmly to her table that day? Would she wait for her at her locker and walk with her to homeroom? Ellen hoped that Maggie would continue to be her sister's friend now that Mr. Ming had been cleared. Suzanne was so sweet and trusting. Ellen couldn't bear to see her hurt.

Maggie was waiting on the sidewalk as the Mings drove up. She waved at Suzanne and ran over to the car and opened the door herself. Her freckled face was full of laughter.

"Suzanne told me the news—congratulations!" she said to Ellen and Mrs. Ming. "I'm Maggie Hoffman," she said, "Suzanne's friend. I'm so happy for your family! I knew Mr. Ming was innocent—everybody at school did."

"How do you do, Maggie?" Mrs. Ming grinned at Maggie's enthusiasm. "And thank you."

"So, Suzanne, will you come to my slumber party on Saturday night, now?" Maggie asked as Suzanne and Ellen got out of the car. She turned to Mrs. Ming. "I asked her already, but she said no because she wanted to stay home with the family. Can she come, Mrs. Ming?"

"Of course," Mrs. Ming said. Her dark

eyes sparkled. "I'm happy to see she's made such a good friend, Maggie."

"I'm glad I finally got up the nerve to talk to her," Maggie admitted with a grin. "I always thought she wouldn't want to talk to me. She's much smarter than I am."

Suzanne punched her lightly on the arm. "No, I'm not," she said. "And, anyway, I couldn't crack a joke to save my life."

"Well, you haven't felt much like cracking jokes lately," Maggie pointed out. "Let's go talk to Jan and Kristi. We're dying to hear all the details of what happened. You should have seen Kim Bishop's face when she got here!"

The two girls ran off, and Ellen got out of the car and said goodbye to her mother. She turned and faltered for a moment. Suddenly it was as though nothing had changed. Kim Bishop was in her usual place by the marble stairs, surrounded by her friends. And Ellen was alone.

But then she saw that Karen and Ben were starting toward her. Also Nikki looked over and waved. She nudged Niles, and then they headed over, followed by Robin, Calvin, and Lacey. Finally more kids swayed toward her—Cheryl Worth and Mark Giordano and Chris Martinez and Martin Salko—and soon Ellen was surrounded by friends. Laughing, they all tried to maneuver up the walk together. Ellen saw Kim quickly turn away and open the door to school. She disappeared from sight.

Nikki slipped next to Ellen. "I called Nancy last night after you called me," she said. "She was really thrilled at the news. And she said not to worry about the other thing. She'll be back in town at the end of next week if we need help. But, hopefully, we won't."

"Great," Ellen said. They couldn't really talk with so many other people around, so Nikki nodded once, to show she'd heard, and changed the subject.

"So are you going to the father-daughter dance tonight?" she asked.

"Gosh, I hadn't even thought about it," Ellen said. "All week I've been dreading hearing about it. But now, I don't know."

"You *have* to come," Robin said bluntly. "How can you resist showing up Kim Bishop and her father? They deserve to be run out of town on a rail, but I'd settle for seeing them really embarrassed."

Ellen giggled. "That's not a bad idea."

"It's a terrific idea," Nikki agreed firmly. "Robin's right. You and your father should be there."

"All right," Ellen agreed, but her mind had already begun to wander. She saw Kevin Hoffman standing over by the bike rack, locking his bike. He raised his head and met her eyes, then quickly glanced down at his lock again.

"Listen, you guys, I'll be right back, okay?" Ellen said. She left the group and hurried across the lawn toward Kevin.

"Hi," she said as she came up.

"Hi," he said. He shifted uneasily and looked over her shoulder. "Listen, Maggie told me about your father," he said uncomfortably. "Suzanne called her last night. I'm happy for you, Ellen."

Ellen smiled shyly. "Thank you, Kevin. Thanks for being nice to me, even though I don't deserve it."

Kevin moved his backpack to his other shoulder. His usually happy, open face looked stern. "I don't know what you mean."

"I think you do," Ellen said softly. "I was very mean to you, Kevin."

Kevin still didn't look her in the eye. "Well," he said stiffly, "I guess you had a lot on your mind."

"That's no excuse," Ellen returned. "You were really great to help out with Suzanne. I was afraid that Maggie was just being nice. I didn't want Suzanne to be hurt in the end. I thought Maggie might drop her after the talk at school died down."

Kevin shook his head. "Maggie would never do that. Look, all I told Maggie was to watch out for Suzanne a little bit, that she was shy. It turned out that Maggie had already wanted to be friends with Suzanne. She thought she was standoffish. Maggie sees Suzanne as this brilliant, talented kid, and she was a little in awe. But now they giggle together like maniacs." Kevin grinned. "They're going to drive me nuts, believe me. So don't worry about Maggie dropping Suzanne. She really likes her. I tried to tell you that."

"I know," Ellen admitted. "I'm afraid I wasn't in the mood to listen. My pride was hurt, I guess."

Kevin looked at her quizzically. "Why?"

"Because you didn't notice me until something bad happened to me, I guess." Ellen said the words in a rush. She felt herself blush, but she made herself go on. "And you were being so nice to me because you felt sorry for me—"

"Felt sorry for you?" Kevin let out a long breath. "Well, yeah, I did—who wouldn't? Your dad got a bum rap. But I wouldn't have asked you out on a date if I just felt sorry for you. I mean," he said with a grin, "I'm not *that* nice, okay?"

"I'm glad to hear it," Ellen said weakly. Did that mean that Kevin really liked her?

He shook his head slowly, staring at her. "You're so pretty," he murmured. Then he stood up straight and said, "So I started to notice you more because of this mess. So what? I finally woke up. There was this beautiful girl sitting across the room from me in student council for months, and I hardly noticed. Call me stupid. Many have."

"This beautiful girl"—Ellen repeated the words in her head. Did he really say that? "Okay, stupid," she said, grinning.

Kevin winced. "I deserved that. Listen," he said awkwardly, "I'm not what you'd call an expert on girl behavior. I'm sorry I made you uncomfortable. But we can just be friends, Ellen. That's okay, too."

Ellen bit her lip to control herself. She wanted to burst out laughing. Suddenly she was so happy! "Maybe you just asked at a bad time," she said softly.

Kevin looked at her, hope lighting his eyes. "I *am* known for my bad timing," he said. "How about tonight, then? Would you like to see a movie or something?"

Disappointment thudded through Ellen. "Oh, I can't. I just told Nikki I'd go to the father-daughter dance at the country club."

"Yeah, well, that sounds like a good idea. Fun and everything." Kevin shifted his backpack to his other shoulder again. He looked down at his feet.

Ellen was surprised. She'd never imagined that Kevin Hoffman could be shy. "How about Saturday?" she asked hesitantly.

Immediately Kevin's face broke into a grin. "Saturday? Saturday is even better!"

Ellen started to laugh, and Kevin joined her. "Even better," she agreed.

On Friday night Brittany was relieved when she came down the stairs and saw her father. Somehow, she'd had a totally irrational vision of him in his old coffee-colored sweater and sneakers. But he looked fantastic in a navy suit and a silk tie.

"You look great, Daddy," she said warmly.

"Thanks, sweetie. You'll be the most beautiful girl there, I'm sure."

Mrs. Tate smiled at both of them. "You'll be the best-looking couple at the dance. Now, don't be too late. I'll be waiting up to hear all about it."

Brittany went to get her coat. She never felt less like doing something in her life. How was she going to keep her father away from the socially important people at the dance? He was sure to embarrass her. He didn't belong to the right organizations or know the right restaurants or anything. And what if Missy talked to him? Brittany would be sunk.

As they drove to the club, Brittany reflected that she had one consolation, at least. She couldn't help feeling a little thrill of anticipation at the thought of Kim facing Ellen and her father. Kim had been humiliated, there was no doubt about it. Everyone at school thought she was a witch. There just might be some fireworks at the dance. For once, Brittany could stand back and watch with a clear conscience.

When they got to the club, Brittany had the bad luck to spot Missy immediately. She was standing next to a tall man with silvered temples. Brittany wished Mr. Henderson didn't look quite so distinguished.

"Come on, Brittany. Let's dance." Her father's foot was tapping appreciatively as the band swung into a fast, bouncy tune.

Brittany almost groaned aloud. Sometimes it was hard to remember that her absentminded father loved to dance. There was hardly anyone on the floor, and they'd look totally conspicuous. "Can we wait a little bit, Dad?" she asked. "I'm covering this for the *Record,* remember, and I should talk to a few girls before everyone starts dancing."

"Sure, pumpkin," her father agreed. He'd better not call her that in front of anyone else! "Oh, there's Mr. Masters. I'll go have a word with him."

Good, Brittany thought. Mr. Masters would be a great person for her father to be seen with, even if he was Nikki's father. Brittany drifted off to look at the flower arrangements. She'd promised her mother she'd make a note of them.

Just then she saw Ellen Ming and her father come in the door. Ellen looked fabulous in a chic jungle-print minidress. Brittany wondered where she got her clothes. Ellen was a sophisticated and stylish dresser, and Brittany never saw her clothes at the mall.

Mr. Ming removed Ellen's winter coat, which was an unusual, gorgeous shade of ice green. Brittany was so busy admiring the coat that she almost missed the Bishops coming through the door. Kim's fair skin flushed, and stout Mr. Bishop suddenly looked as though his shirt was too tight. He yanked nervously at his collar.

Fireworks! Brittany thought. Quickly she headed toward the group. There was no way she'd miss this confrontation!

13 

Ellen saw the Bishops before her father did. She stared coolly at Kim. That girl would never make Ellen drop her eyes again.

This time, it was Kim who dropped her eyes. Mr. Ming had his hand on Ellen's elbow, and he squeezed it gently. "Let's find our table, Ellen," he said in a low tone.

But then Mr. Bishop cleared his throat and came forward awkwardly. "I'm glad to have a chance to see you face-to-face, David," he said. "I hope all is forgiven." He stuck out his hand.

Mr. Ming hesitated, staring at Mr. Bishop. Ellen wondered what her father would do. Would he forgive the man who'd hurt him and his family so badly, who'd rushed to slander his name before the facts were known?

Finally Mr. Ming did shake Mr. Bishop's hand, but he didn't say a word.

Now it was Kim's turn. She was rooted to the spot, staring at her father speechlessly. She seemed shocked at what he'd done, and she didn't seem ready to apologize to Ellen in the least.

Around her, Ellen felt people stir. She saw Nikki and her father, Robin and Lacey with their fathers, Samantha and Mr. Daley, Cheryl and Mr. Worth. She saw friends and strangers, and they all were staring at Kim. Waiting.

Ellen saw Mr. Bishop's neck flush an angry red next to his snowy white collar. He put a hand on his daughter's shoulder. "I think you have something to say to Ellen, don't you, Kimberly?"

Kim came forward with tiny steps. "I'm sorry," she mumbled.

Ellen inclined her head. "Excuse me?"

"I said I'm sorry," Kim said in a louder voice. "I apologize for all the things I said. I was wrong."

"Thank you," Ellen said simply. Then she turned and took her father's arm. Everyone stepped back to clear a path. Ellen and her father smiled at each other, then walked in to the ballroom with their heads held high. Behind them, the rest of the people filed in, leaving Kim and Mr. Bishop to trail behind.

But even at that moment, amid all her happiness, Ellen couldn't forget what lay ahead. That night she'd enjoy her father, and Saturday night she had a date with Kevin. The weekend would be fantastic.

But come Monday morning, she'd have to face her biggest problem. Preparations for the luau would begin. She'd have to write checks, she'd have to answer request after request from the luau committee—money for food, additional decorations, last-minute items. And she didn't have the money for any of it. The pressure was building. Ellen had to find the thief—fast!

"That was some scene," Brittany said to Samantha later while their fathers talked about pro basketball. "Kim really blew it this time. She's going to have to wear a paper bag on her head when she comes back to school."

"Well, at least she apologized," Samantha said doubtfully.

"You call that an apology? Her father practically had to pull teeth to get it out of her," Brittany gloated. "I wouldn't blame Ellen if she made Kim's name mud at school."

"Ellen's not like that. That's the difference between her and Kim," Samantha said matter-of-factly. "I'm just glad it's all over. Now I'll start worrying about you, Brittany."

"Me?" Brittany asked, surprised. "I'm doing great."

"Mmmm," Samantha murmured skeptically. "Tell me, would the fact that you're doing great have anything to do with why that little blond preppie person over there is staring daggers at you?"

Brittany didn't even have to turn around to know who Samantha was talking about. She winced. "You noticed?"

"Hon, it's hard to miss," Samantha drawled in her honeyed accent. "She'd poison your food if she could. This wouldn't have anything to do with Chip Worthington, would it?"

"I'm afraid so," Brittany said.

Samantha frowned. "Is he really worth it? Kim says he's an awful snob."

"It takes one to know one," Brittany returned promptly. "Kim and Jeremy are a hundred times worse than Chip. He can be sweet, Samantha. You just don't know him." Hidden in the folds of her old blue taffeta dress were Brittany's crossed fingers. Chip Worthington wasn't exactly *sweet*. But when you had rich and socially prominent, who cared about sweet?

Samantha's father and Mr. Tate finished their conversation and came over. Samantha's handsome father smiled at her. "Samantha, you've hardly talked to your father tonight. What do you say to a dance?"

"With the handsomest father in the room, I say yes, of course," Samantha said, touching her father's sleeve.

Brittany rolled her eyes. Unbelievable. Samantha flirted even with her father. The girl was hopeless.

Samantha leaned over as she drifted by. "Put your phaser on stun, girl," she murmured.

"What do you—" Brittany stopped her question abruptly when she twisted around and saw Missy approaching on her father's arm. "Daddy, let's go get some punch," Brittany said, grabbing her father's arm.

"We just had some," Mr. Tate protested.

"I want some more."

"Well, I've finally caught up to you." Brittany heard the simpering voice behind her and closed her eyes. It was too late now. She turned and smiled at the Hendersons.

"Hi, Missy."

"Daddy, this is a new friend of mine, Brittany Tate. Brittany, my father, Brooks Henderson."

"How do you do?" Brittany said graciously. "And this is my father, James Tate."

The two men shook hands while Missy smiled sweetly at Brittany. "Enjoying the dance?" she asked.

"It's great," Brittany said. "We haven't had a chance to dance much, though, so—"

"Mr. Tate," Missy interrupted, turning to Brittany's father. "I've been wondering. You wouldn't be related to the Philadelphia Tates, would you?"

"Sorry," Mr. Tate said amiably.

"I know," Mr. Henderson said. "The Charleston Tates. Trish and Bill?"

Her father's brown eyes gleamed with mischief. Brittany's heart sank into her pumps. She knew what was coming.

"Actually," he said, "I hail from the Sioux City Tates."

Mr. Henderson looked puzzled. "I don't think I've met them."

"We're rather an anonymous bunch," Mr. Tate said seriously. But he quickly winked at Brittany. She wanted to sink through the floor. Mr. Tate obviously thought the Hendersons were ridiculous.

Of course, they were. But she silently begged him not to continue teasing them.

"I don't think I've seen you around the club," Mr. Henderson continued. "What's your game?"

"My game?" Mr. Tate looked puzzled.

"Golf or tennis?"

"Scrabble," Mr. Tate said with a grin. "My younger daughter, Tamara, beats me every time, though."

"I see," Mr. Henderson said. He took a step backward. "I think I'll get a drink from the bar," he told Missy.

"I'll join you," Mr. Tate said.

"Right," Mr. Henderson said with a pained smile.

Brittany sighed as the two men walked off. Her father was hopeless. He was just too down-to-earth to care about making any kind of an impression. In sixty seconds he'd destroyed any illusion she might create for Chip that her family had even an ounce of social standing.

"Your father has quite a sense of humor," Missy said, her mouth twisting in amusement as she watched the two men approach the bar. Mr. Tate looked positively disheveled next to Mr. Henderson's polish. "He's super," Missy said. There was the slightest trace of mockery in her voice.

Anger shot through Brittany. She wanted to wipe that smile off Missy's face, preferably with a good right cross. But right crosses were too direct for someone like Missy. Brittany knew how to deal with her. She shrugged. "My father's a brilliant scientist," she said, "so he's a bit eccentric. What does your father do, Missy?"

"He doesn't work," Missy said smugly.

"Oh, I'm sorry," Brittany said, widening her eyes in fake concern. "Can't find a job?"

"He doesn't *have* to work," Missy said, flushing with anger. "He handles the family's investments. I guess that's something that's completely out of your realm, Brittany."

"Yes, I'm more used to people who contribute to society. But I'm sure your father's golf game is really tops," Brittany said. But maybe she shouldn't have. Missy looked really furious now.

Missy took a step toward Brittany. Her moon-shaped face had two bright patches of red on her cheeks. "I know what you're up to, Brittany Tate," she spat out in a low, furious tone. "Chip canceled our date for tomorrow night, and I know very well why. My friend Tracy saw you with him at the club last night."

"It's a free country," Brittany said, flicking a nonexistent speck off her dress. "And if you can't keep your boyfriend, Missy, I don't know how I can possibly help you. I'm not about to give you lessons, you know."

Missy's pale blue eyes gleamed with malice. "Then I'll give *you* a lesson, Brittany. Chip might date you once or twice. But he'll never be serious about you."

Brittany felt a prick of fear at the back of her neck. But she couldn't let Missy see that she'd unnerved her. "All right, Missy," she said with exaggerated patience. "I *will* give you a hint. I'd ditch that dress if I were you. Bright green looks really bad on you."

Missy caught her thin lower lip in her teeth and gave Brittany a hard look. "I'd think about what I said if I were you. You see, anybody can buy a country club membership, Brittany. But not everybody can *belong.*"

Missy turned on one heel and was gone, her green dress swirling. As soon as she'd turned her back, Brittany collapsed into a chair. All her strength had left her body, and she felt a little dizzy.

Brittany looked around at the crowd. So many of the girls looked like Missy clones. Their hair was straight and parted on the side, they wore pastels and low-heeled shoes. Brittany knew she stuck out like a sore thumb in her blue taffeta dress. She didn't fit in with those girls, it was true.

What if Missy was right? Hadn't Kim warned her that Chip wasn't a nice person? He could use her and then drop her. Suddenly Brittany shuddered. She would have to be very, very careful. Chip Worthington could turn her into the laughingstock of the country club, not to mention the whole town!

Will Ellen find out who's been dipping into the junior-class funds before she's accused of being the thief? A sophomore has a major crush on Robin, and she's not exactly discouraging him. Could this mean the end of her romance with Calvin? Find out in River Heights #10, *Mixed Emotions*.